Who's Killing Aphrodite's
Priestesses: 1st Chronicles

Kat Burquette

Who's Killing Aphrodite's Priestesses: 1st Chronicles

Chimera

CHIMERA PAPERBACK

© Copyright 2025
Kat Burquette

A CIP catalogue record for this title is
available from the British Library.

ISBN 978-1-915451-12-5

Chimera is an imprint of
Pegasus Elliot MacKenzie Publishers Ltd.
www.pegasuspublishers.com

First Published in 2025

Chimera
Sheraton House Castle Park
Cambridge England

Printed & Bound in Great Britain

Dedication

This book is dedicated to the concept of a gentler, kinder, more maternalistic society.

Prologue

My name is Mary Ellyn Cartwright, and I am a priestess of Aphrodite at a lovemaking academy called Fantasy Bay, located at an all-inclusive resort on the west coast of Panama.

What, you might ask, is a lovemaking academy?

Our students are taught advanced lovemaking techniques and actually practice them with real teachers. Male students have real women called priestesses as their teachers. Female students' teachers are real men called priests. Teaching people to be good lovers, good partners, and the principals of the Divine Feminine is what we do here at Fantasy Bay. We are quite good at it, as you will see.

Chapter One

I was walking along the beach toward my lifelong friend Shannel's bungalow. Once we met up, we were headed to our daily martial arts session, and after that, we were to hook up with our students to practice today's lovemaking lesson, *Advanced Cunnilingus,* with them.

Compared to what most guys do, cunnilingus done the way we teach it, is like the difference between professional sports and high school sports. Classes like *Advanced Cunnilingus* and then having guys practice with us afterwards were normal mornings for Shannel and me. As I approached her bungalow, I suddenly stopped in my tracks. An unusual aura was emanating from Shannel's bungalow, and I knew what it meant.

Danger Close!

One thing to know about all priestesses of Aphrodite is that we are well trained in the Zen based martial art known as Tae Kwon Do. The Divine Feminine, whom we call Aphrodite, wants women to be able to stand up for themselves physically. We've all been told that we can't. 'Men are stronger and we can't win a fight with a guy.' This is a lie perpetrated by people who wish to keep women subservient. Any sixteen-year-old girl well-trained in Tae Kwon Do can stand up to any grown man. We do have to work harder at this, but it can be done; that is the truth, and I am living proof of this.

The reason why this is one of Aphrodite's principals for women has a lot to it. Obviously, when a woman choses to say "no," she should be able to make it stick, but there is more to it than that. When a woman can stand up for herself physically, it empowers her to stand up for what she believes in any other way she wants to as well. There are no female martial artists in need of empowerment.. We are the definition of power, and this is also true of Aphrodite's priestesses. The Divine Feminine has gifts for women, and those of us who develop the skill to use them are empowered as well. We are wonderful partners for men, but as equals. None ever dominate us. This is who we are, who Aphrodite intended all women to be.

I am "Sam Dan," which means I am a Third Degree Black Belt. Many of Aphrodite's priestesses have completed this level of martial arts training, and yes, I can break boards with my hands and feet. That's easy. Any fourteen-year-old girl can learn this in about six months if she wants. More importantly, it is not possible to surprise someone like me. Our Sam Dan training is extensive in this area. Our sensei blindfolds us and throws punches and kicks, which we cannot see, and we have to sense and block them. In time, with a lot of training, we learn to feel danger that we cannot see. There it was again.

Danger Close!

The sudden change in the aura surrounding her bungalow was unmistakable and the sensation exploded into my senses. This sensation of danger wafts into your senses just like the stench when someone farts. We have a name for this sensation:

Danger Close!

…But I'm getting ahead of the story.

***

Our priesthood has decided it is my task to begin telling our story, a story that has been kept secret for many years. We have intentionally stayed under the radar for over a decade, but recent events now require our story to be told. This is Shannel's story, my story, and the story of the priestesses and priests of Aphrodite.

The mission of our priesthood is to teach people how to be great lovers, great life partners, and foster an understanding of the principles of the Divine Feminine. We honor the Divine Masculine in all of its manifestations, but much focus is already placed there. We focus on the feminine side of the heavens. We do this at two places, one of which is Fantasy Bay, about an hour north of Panama City, Panama, located at an all-inclusive tropical resort on a pristine bay on the west coast of Panama, and the other is Fantasy Valley, an all-inclusive mountain resort outside of Portillo, Chile. Both are literally love-making academies, but don't bother looking for us on maps… you won't find any reference to us there.

If you are intending to come to us, when you arrive, you will discover a large, lovely bay with a number of islands and numerous reefs, a beautiful broad beach bordered by dunes resplendent with tropical foliage, delightful lagoon-linked pools, and pristine nature walks in a lush tropical rain forest. There is a marina with sailboats, ski boats, and jet skis that allow guests to engage in water sports or make their way out to the islands for sexy picnics in the bay. There are dive boats that take guests out to beautiful coral reefs with multitudes of colorful fish and anemones that are only hinted at from the surface but create a panoramic seascape of unparalleled beauty for a diver. In short, Fantasy Bay is a tropical paradise. But finding us is hard… by design.

What we believe and what we do is somewhat unconventional. In this day and time, unconventional means controversial, which often also means dangerous. We do not advertise. Reservations at our resort are by invitation only.

The feminine side of God has been called by many names throughout human history. Dan Brown called her the 'Sacred Feminine.' Cultural anthropologists believe that in European pre-history she may have been known as the 'Great Earth Mother,' the Greeks knew her as both 'Aphrodite' and 'Hera,' the Romans called her 'Venus,' the Hindus still call her 'Lakshmi.' Jewish people, as well as those Christians with a deep knowledge of the Old Testament know her as 'El Shaddai' (which means the God with breasts in Hebrew and is often translated as 'God Almighty'.) References to the feminine side of God are salted through the New Testament as well, so there is nothing new or sacrilegious about the Divine Feminine. At Fantasy Bay we simply call her Aphrodite.

Many benefits can accrue to a couple who lives their lives well-seasoned by Aphrodite. A couple is practically impossible to break up or hold back when they follow her ways of making love. Such a couple becomes one with each other in ways that do not otherwise occur, stronger, happier, indivisible, and this makes them happier and more successful. By whatever name you choose to call her, 'happier and more successful' exemplifies the Divine Feminine in action.

The men and women we accept have to be at the right place in their lives to come here: intelligent, competent, and open-minded, most of all, understanding the world is full of things to learn, particularly about women. But even if you are not yet meant to come to us, the precepts and principles we teach are presented throughout these Chronicles. If your heart is open, this series of books will give you the keys to an advanced knowledge of the Divine Feminine. If you decide to take the keys presented here, open the locks and walk through Aphrodite's doors; the possibilities are endless.

This Chronicle is Shannel's story and my story. To tell it properly, I should begin with the beginning. Everything began for us ten years ago, in high school, actually. Shannel and I were high school cheerleaders together. It's where our friendship began. Our besties bond was forged almost immediately. I was interested in a guy named Brad, and she was hot for his best friend Jack. With Brad, I got really lucky. Jack's older sister had taught Brad what to do with a girl who was giving him her cherry. This is supposed to be a joyful thing for a girl, and yes, there is some pain, but a guy who knows what to do with a virgin girl can get her through it quickly, and on to a place where she can really enjoy her first time. Jack's older sister had taught Brad what to do with girls by literally having him do it with her.

My first time began with wonderful foreplay, then came some pain that did not last long, and ended with a terrific orgasm, and I have loved sex from that first time until now. Brad made sure I had a wonderful orgasm, and the other neat thing he did was share how to do all of this with Jack. He'd learned it from Jack's sister after all, but I don't think he ever told Jack who it was who taught him. LOL! Jack made sure Shannel enjoyed losing her cherry too. We had them for a year and then they were off to college. Our high school years were filled with short skirts, high kicks and boys, but even then, we were on the priestess track. You see, a girl who cared about girls a lot had taught our guys what to do with us.

Next came college. The end goal of high school had always been college. We lived in Tennessee, but Shannel and I were tired of the Tennessee landscape and decided to go to the University of Miami and room together. The Florida Keys were where we fell in love with beaches. We particularly loved taking a guy back out of sight in the soft sand of the dunes and having your way with him under the silver light of the moon. I had always been fascinated by the light of the moon, most girls are, but it would be years before I would find out why. This is one of Aphrodite's secrets, but in the fullness of time, I did learn why we love the moon, and so will you.

What was the end goal after college? Neither of us had a clue. The first thing about college was that it was harder, mostly because you need to be interested in learning what they're teaching. Neither of us really were. We were just going through the motions without any real plan. Both of us majored in business, and it's true, we liked the idea of owning a small business one day. We talked of being partners in a bake shop, but how were we ever going to get the money to start one? We had prepared a business plan for the bakery in our senior year and knew we needed about two hundred thousand dollars. Our best plan was to take jobs in the same town, see where they led, and save our money. We had narrowed things down to Ft. Lauderdale and Sarasota.

In the spring of our senior year, we decided to do Spring Break at an all-inclusive resort in Panama. The two of us were walking down the concourse to get our luggage in the Panama City Airport when I spotted a woman holding a sign that said:

Like Panama?
High-paying careers
for well educated
attractive women

I looked at Shannel who smiled and nodded, so I walked over. The lady with the sign smiled as I approached. "Well," she began, "you are certainly attractive enough, stunning in fact. Your friend is too. Are you here for Spring Break?"

15

"Yes," I answered a little guardedly. "What's this about?"

"My name is Regina. I work for a woman named Helena," she began. "She is the chief staff instructor at Fantasy Bay, an all-inclusive resort about forty-five minutes away. This is about jobs that pay two hundred thousand dollars a year," she replied.

My eyes widened, and I looked at her. "Two hundred thousand! Is this legal?" I blurted out. I could tell the same thoughts were going through Shannel's mind as my own. If this was legal, it might be the ticket to saving the money we needed for the bakery.

"Yes," she answered with a laugh and handed me a card that said Fantasy Bay Resort. "Why don't you get checked into your resort. Call me and I'll send a car. Helena will explain everything."

That was one moment that really changed our lives. More were to come.

We arrived at Fantasy Bay about three hours later. The car drove down a flowering bougainvillea-lined terracotta brick road toward a beautiful Italian-style building and pulled under a portico. Two bellmen came up immediately and opened the doors. We went inside, and Regina introduced us to Helena in the foyer.

"Welcome," she said simply. "Please follow me."

She led us out a set of large double glass doors toward a pool area. The first thing that we remembered noticing was the tropical beauty of the scene laid out before us. Bougainvillea and Hibiscus bushes were everywhere. The broad fronds of a cluster of Queen Palm trees shaded a nearby pool. The layout was lush and lavish, but that is where the resemblance to an upscale resort ended and something else began. A woman was reclining in a lounge chair under an umbrella, near the pool. She was gorgeous… and… she was nude. A man walked up in a G-string with two drinks. He was just as gorgeous and practically as nude. He settled into the lounge next to her and handed her one of the drinks.

I looked off in another direction and saw another couple holding drinks and talking in one of the palm shaded pool's cul-de-sacs. The water was up to their knees, and both of them were also nude.

Obviously, a million questions were running through our heads when we sat down in Helena's office.

"Is this a brothel?" I asked, coming straight to the point.

"No." Helena laughed.

"A nudist colony?" Shannel asked.

"Sorry, wrong again," she answered with a smile.

"Come sort of religious cult?" I asked.

"No, girls… Fantasy Bay is a lovemaking academy," Helena replied with a smile in her voice.

"A… what!" Shannel exclaimed and then shook her head in disbelief. "No … there is no such thing!"

Helena threw back her head and laughed out loud. "Oh, yes, there is. We teach people how to be great lovers and great partners."

"Really?" I asked, but it was more a statement than a question. She looked at us carefully.

"Really!" Helena nodded. "You see, most men are clueless about women. They don't mean to be, but they are, and women have gotten so used to it we accept this as normal." She paused and looked at me. "Can you tell me that when you are having sex, men know much about what you want, or even care? Or do they just do what they want... hoping you like it too?"

I thought about this. It was true; they all pretty much did their own thing. "No," I answered. "You're right, but I like it too, a lot, so it's not like they're being mean or anything."

"Of course not," Helena nodded and continued, "But guys could be so much better. For example, have you ever had a guy start things by taking the time to slowly savor the essence of your femininity as if it were a fine wine to be leisurely cherished?"

She paused and looked at us and went on, "Have you known a guy to care enough about your pleasure to move slowly enough, deep enough, so you felt his every thrust through to the center of your soul?" She smiled, almost sadly, because she knew the answer.

"Have you ever had a guy, after his orgasm was over, to finish by staying in you and taking a lovely long time to gently relish the incomparable luxury of tender intimacy with you?"

As she spoke, I knew she was describing something I had never dared to consider, but that she had actually experienced. I thought about this, and realized her words resonated from a place deep in her soul to a place deep within my own soul.

"A guy starting things by taking the time to slowly savor the essence of my femininity as if it were a fine wine to be leisurely cherished

... caring enough for my pleasure to move slowly enough, deep enough, so that I felt his every thrust through to the center of my soul

... to finish by staying in me and taking a lovely long time to gently relish the incomparable luxury of tender intimacy with me."

Just thinking about something like that brought tears to my eyes. The answer was no. There had never been a guy who felt this way about me. What would it feel like to be in someone's arms and share with each other what Helena had described?

Dear God in Heaven that must be nice. But the truth was, I had no idea what something like that might be like.

"No," I finally answered, a little sadly as my eyes teared up. "No one has ever been anything like that with me." I found myself choking up a little bit. "I didn't know guys could even imagine something like you described. Are you really serious? A real guy will actually be like that with a real girl? This is what you teach here?"

"Yes, and yes," Helena assured us gently with a soft, kind tone to her voice, "Guys who have been taught the ways of the Divine Feminine are actually like this all the time. It's part of what we teach. They have learned how to be like that."

"Really?" I replied, thoughtfully, with a distinctly wishful tone to my voice. This was a revelation.

"Yes," Helena answered tenderly, as if speaking with a younger sister, "Mary Ellyn, what I just described is the way the Divine Feminine intended men to be with us."

"Divine Feminine?" Shannel asked. The wishful quality in her voice was clear too. "Like the Sacred Feminine in the "DaVinci Code?"

"Yes, exactly," Helena continued, "The idea that there is a God the Father, and a God the Son, and ignoring that this means there must be a God the Mother is misogynistic insanity we don't tolerate. But here at Fantasy Bay, we call the feminine part of the Godhead, "Aphrodite," after the Greek Goddess of Making Love. Everything we teach here originates from a feminine perspective. Aphrodite's input animates everything we do. For example, our teachers who train men how to love women… are all women."

Shannel shook her head in disbelief. "Wait a second. You have women teaching men how to love women."

"Very well trained women, yes," Helena just smiled, "We call these women priestesses. This is what I hope you guys will choose to become."

Shannel and I looked at each other, remembering our first times with Brad and his best friend Jack. Brad had been taught by Jack's older sister, but she had taught him well by having sex with him.

"And they do this teaching," Shannel continued, "Without having sex with them? How?"

"By making real love with them," Helena answered. "There's a really big difference between having sex and making love."

"But both involve sexual intercourse? Correct?" Shannel continued. "How does a… priestess… someone dedicated to God, do this?"

"Well," Helena chuckled, "You asked two really good questions, and there is a lot to unpack here. Religious leaders have made premarital sex sinful, but the question is: has God? We don't think so. Fornication is defined as an immoral sexual act, but morality evolves over time. In biblical times it was one thing. The moral requirements of that age were rooted in the reality of that time but do not apply today, so premarital sex is not immoral now. You know how you feel when you look out at a majestic scene? A beautiful mountain valley for example and you feel closer to God? When you've actually experienced the heights that you can go with a man who knows what he is doing, you will feel the same way about the Divine Feminine. Both women and men have the same reaction. Our priestesses and priests are simply facilitating people learning about her."

"Wow!" I blurted out unconsciously.

"Next," Helena smiled, "How else is a guy going to experience the joy of savoring a girl's femininity without a real girl letting him savor her? And just so you know, 'savoring' sometimes begins with your clothes on, but it never ends there. And how else is a guy going to learn to take a girl to higher heavens than she's ever imagined, if he's never been shown the way there by a real girl?"

That gave us pause. There was a lot to unpack. "Could you repeat that?" I asked. Helena smiled gently and graciously went over it all again.

"Higher heavens?" Shannel finally asked.

Helena nodded, "Aphrodite has more for you girls than you can imagine right now. And it all starts with men."

"But didn't you say they are the problem?" Shannel asked.

"Yes," Helena nodded, "But it's not because they can't or won't, it's because they don't know how. Making love well is an art form, but it can be taught to any man who wants to truly love a woman. The women who teach this art to guys are very well trained. We call them priestesses of Aphrodite."

"Well trained women, teaching real men, about real women... " Shannel trailed off wistfully, and I knew her mind was reflecting back on how lucky we'd gotten with Brad and Jack.

"That's revolutionary," I blurted out.

"We think so, but here's the deal... it works," Helena continued, "And it works because we are not teaching guys about sex, but instead, we are teaching them how to make love, a specific kind of love we call *Eros* love, and how to do this very well."

She paused for a sip of water, and continued, "Making *Eros* love with us instead of just having sex with us changes everything—"

"And our job," Shannel interrupted, "Would be to teach them how to make love to us?"

Helena smiled again. "Yes, but you see, the way you phrase the question illustrates part of the problem, Shannel. Men aren't ever going to be good at making love if they are doing it... 'to'... you. Great lovers make love... 'with'... you. It is an equal partnership that flows both ways."

"Hmmmm, Okkkk," I thought to myself, nodding and then spoke up, careful not to Blurt this time. "You clearly know a great deal about this, Helena. One thing you

mentioned was a difference between having sex and making love. Could you explain the difference?"

"Certainly," Helena replied with an impressive offhand confidence as if this were an easy question. It may be easy for her, but not for me. I had been wondering about this for a long time.

"Having sex," she explained, "is rooted in the physical, and primarily the gratification of yourself. Sex is so enthralling that a guy can have fun using you to take care of himself, while you are having fun using him to take care of yourself, and you both... do... have fun and both of you get your basic needs met. The truly sad thing is most people never get any farther than this. They never touch more than the surface."

"You realize," Shannel interjected, "You're talking about us?"

"Of course," Helena answered with an incredibly kind and softly sad look in her eyes.

"But if I'm hearing you correctly," I observed, "You are saying it does not have to be this way?"

"Yes, that is exactly what I am saying," Helena took another sip of water and went on, "Aphrodite has more pleasure available for women than you can imagine, but let's continue. Our understanding of "having sex" as opposed to "making love" grew out of Greek concepts. In the Greek language there are nine words that are all translated into the English catchall word "Love." The three that pertain the most to romantic relationships are *Agape, Eros* and *Philia*."

"*Philia* is affectionate love that begins with a physical and romantic attraction. Basically, *Philia* is just casual sex.

We find nothing wrong with this except it could be so much more."

Shannel and I nodded.

"*Eros* love on the other hand," she continued after another sip of water, "Begins with a physical and romantic attraction like *Philia* but does not end there. It includes two more parts, first an emotional connection, and then each partner being committed to the other's pleasure. *Eros* love is selfless in that way. It includes a strong emotional connection and commitment to each other's pleasure but does not include the idea of permanence. What is different about the Greek concept of *Eros* love is that it does not have to last for more than a night and is still real love. These Greek ideas from two thousand years ago track very well with what we consider to be moral behavior today."

Helena smiled at us both and went on, "*Eros* love is Aphrodite's intermediate step that leads to *Agape* love which is the unconditionally committed love which forms the foundation for a permanent relationship. Permanence is a foundational part of *Agape* love. Typically, *Agape* love grows from *Eros* love, but for most successful couples, the sexual component of their relationship started with *Eros* love. *Agape* love comes along later. *Agape* also refers to the unconditional love of God, which is why we refer to the love of a couple in a permanent relationship as *Eros* + *Agape* love."

Once again, she paused to let things sink in and then continued. "*Eros* love is where most good relationships really begin. Physical attraction, strong emotional connection, and selfless commitment to your partner's pleasure… that's *Eros* love. When you both have all that going on, you are truly making *Eros* love, not just having sex. This is what priestesses do with their students. They are not having sex; they are making *Eros* love."

She paused and looked at us. "And then we add in advanced lovemaking techniques that take a couple's real pleasure far higher than their best fantasies. Understanding Aphrodite's ways of love can take you beyond anything you have ever dreamed of."

That comment gave us both pause as we considered it. "And that is what you teach here?" Shannel asked in astonishment.

"Yes," Helena concluded.

Shannel and I were speechless. This was brilliant! I looked at my friend. "Wow" was all I could say at first.

Helena continued. "The total training period is two months, but quite frankly, it starts with the women we recruit to become priestesses really liking to have sex with men. If you do, you will find it easy to learn what we teach, and you will love what we do here. If not... well... I will take you back to the car, and you can get on with your vacation." She looked at us carefully and smiled. "Are you interested?" She already knew the answer.

Both of us nodded. We were in.

Chapter Two

So, the first part of our story ended with us agreeing to join Fantasy Bay, and the second began with what we call priestess training.

At Fantasy Bay, the priestesses of Aphrodite don't do what would normally be considered religious ceremonies. There are no specific religious services or chants, no rituals or hymns. What we do is different. Sometimes we are alone, sometimes with a lover. We stand in a pristine place like a beach or a forest, nude under the moon, gazing up to heaven, drinking in the soft silver light, and opening ourselves up to the Heavens. We've all heard about a woman's intuition, feminine clairvoyance and things like that. We believe these things are actually Aphrodite speaking to women. Spending time drinking in the moonlight is how a woman feeds her intuition, makes Aphrodite's voice stronger, more clear. We call a woman's intuition that has been enhanced like this 'Aphrodite Intuition.' If a priestess of Aphrodite brings a man along, after their time communing with the heavens, they honor their Creator by making glorious *Eros* love under the stars in the amorous heavenly aura two connected people can create. This makes a priestess's connection to Aphrodite, the Goddess of Making Love, even stronger.

Maybe this sort of thing qualifies as a religious ceremony for others, maybe not, but it does for me. Will it for you? Try it sometime. I've never felt closer to heaven than when making *Eros* love on the beach under the light of a silver moon. There are several churches in the town of El Corizon del Bosque which is near the resort, and most of us attend now and then, but communing nude with the heavens, letting the unexplainable wonder of the cosmos wind its way into your soul, and then making true *Eros* love in the moonlight is the only sort of ceremony we participate in as "priestesses." It should go without saying we do this quite often. Over time, my Aphrodite Intuition has become extremely strong, and I've learned I can rely on it a lot.

Once Shannel and I had gone home, told our friends and families we were joining an all-inclusive resort as "teachers," we returned to Panama. Neither set of parents particularly liked this idea, but we were both over twenty-one, so they didn't really have much they could do about it.

We were picked up at the Panama City Airport and flown to the resort by helicopter. Once we got to the resort, the first thing on the agenda was a tour, which turned out to be the reason for the helicopter. The pilot flew, and the guy in the copilot seat was the tour guide. Fantasy Bay was built on a bay with a spectacular white sand beach on Panama's west coast. It faces west, and no matter what season of the year, there is always a place on the beach where you can see a glorious sunset.

Out in the Bay were three good-sized islands and a scattering of smaller ones. Just inland from the beach was a section of barrier dunes with palm trees, beach grasses, and sea grapes. We could see a number of covered pavilions and Tiki Bars, two of which were right on the edge between the beach and the dunes.

"Wow," Shannel had remarked, "I bet you have a great view of the sunsets from those Bars."

"Right," I agreed. "I wonder how the food is?"

"Outstanding," the pilot remarked. "Everything here is good, but the seafood is simply world-class."

The copilot grinned. "Everything served here this evening was swimming yesterday afternoon. We have our own fishing boats. They fish all night and dock at eight in the morning."

In from the dunes were the pools. Fantasy Bay had nine.

A bit farther inland were bungalows. Two hundred according to the copilot.

"That's where you will be living," he explained. "Each of you will have your own."

"Where do the guests stay?" I asked.

"With you," he answered. "One is assigned to each of you. He is often called your Mon Chéri. You are often called his Ma Chérie. Your Mon Chéri will spend the nights and attend a morning class with you. After the class, you go back to your bungalow together and practice what the lesson was about, but this will all be explained at your orientation."

"The two arcs of the pools," he explained, "are traced by the bungalows. This leaves a lot of space in between. Those buildings in the central area are called the Village. There are three more restaurants: The Crystal Martini, which specializes in steaks and seafood, and the Cuisine

L'Europe, which is French. They have the best Fillet of Sole I've ever had. Their Chateaubriand will change your religion. The third is Selva Tropical Gourmet and has terrific Mexican and Spanish food. Over there," he said, pointing at the last building, "is where the training auditorium and all of the offices are."

"Beyond all of this you will see the rainforest," he indicated. "There are five outstanding nature trails. The biodiversity is astonishing. The beauty is breathtaking."

The helicopter landed and we were escorted to our individual bungalows. These were one-bedroom suites, each with a living area complete with a Kitchenette / Dinette, a spacious Bedroom, and a really nice Bath that included a Jacuzzi and a magnificent two-headed shower.

Outside, in a fenced area surrounded by lush palms and fragrant flowering bushes, was a small private pool with a reclined seat built-in at one end. I smiled because I had a pretty good idea what that was about. I walked back in. "Nice," I said aloud to the bathroom as I unpacked my toiletries. "Really, really nice."

They assigned each of us a priestess, and the one assigned to me was named Debbie. She arrived at my bungalow precisely at ten with some luggage, which she left on the bed. We sat down in the living area, and Debbie began with something I didn't expect.

"My first job," she said with a serious smile, "Is to make sure you are up to speed on a few things quickly. The first is female anatomy, what your girl parts are called here at the Bay, and a few other basic principles."

"Excuse me?" I said. After all, I am a girl, why on earth would I need the names of my girl parts explained?

Debbie nodded, "You probably think it's weird that we need to talk about this, but the prudish nature of society has conditioned women to be embarrassed talking about this stuff. This limits the info available to most women. Maybe you know all of this already, and if you do, I promise to apologize, but maybe you don't, so let's just go through this quickly. OK?"

I nodded.

"First," she continued, "The Divine Feminine created women for a lot of things, one of which is sex."

She gave me a very direct look. "Period."

She looked at me for a second, and continued, "Having sex with men is certainly not the only thing women were created for, but just as certainly, sexuality is a significant piece of a woman's identity. No one is ever complete until they embrace all aspects of their true selves. For uncommitted girls this means embracing both their physical and their emotional sexuality. When a woman learns how to embrace them both... well... it inevitably results in her making *Eros* love with guys often. We view this as a good thing."

"Moving on to the terminology we use here, the visible part of your genital anatomy we call your Pussy. Your Venus Mons is where your pubic hair would be if you still have any, the Groove is the slot in your Pussy formed by your Labia, your Clitoris we call your Hot Spot, the entrance to your Vagina is called your Intro, your Vagina itself we also call your Pussy, your Anus we call your Ass."

She looked at me and continued, "Now, a lot of women do not like the word 'Pussy.' This reticence is related to the prudes of society not wanting women to embrace their sexuality. We do not have this problem around here. Vagina is a clinical term, and there should be nothing clinical about making love. Same with men, we use the term Cock, not penis for the same reason. A man's pubic bone over his Cock is called the Hilt."

"Your Pussy begins with your Intro. It's where a man Introduces his Cock to your Pussy. As you move in, next is your G- spot, which is up about an inch and a half on your front side, then up another half an inch is your A-spot. These two are close together and normally stimulated together so here they are lumped together and just called the G spot. Up about four inches from your Intro is your Cervix. Attached to your Cervix is your O-spot. We call the natural lubricant your Pussy produces "Aphrodite's Nectar.""

She looked at me again to see if I was keeping up. I was.

"Next, a girl has four orgasmic zones. These are nerve collections which are capable of producing an orgasm by themselves. The first one is the Hot Spot, the next is your Intro, then the G Spot. The last is your O-Spot."

"Now, a lot of times guys do not manage to stimulate the G-spot, and girls miss a lot of joy as a result. The G-spot is on the top side of your Pussy and easily stimulated by a man's finger if he takes the time to find it, but the only way a guy's Cock can stimulate it is for the Head to ride up against the top of your Pussy as it passes during his thrust. The way this is done is for you to spread your legs really wide which allows his hips to ride low, and then for him to understand he needs to keep them low during his thrust. This makes his Cock ride the low side of your Intro during his thrust, which levers the head of his Cock up against the top side of your Pussy and stimulates your G-spot very nicely, and just so you know, there is nothing you or a man can do with fingers which is nearly as satisfying for a women as doing it with his Cock."

"A guy's erect Cock is over five and a half inches long. So, if you spread your legs wide enough so he can thrust all of the way into you, his Cock presses on your Cervix and stretches out your Pussy to the size of his Cock. This process of his Cock pressing on your Cervix and stretching out your Pussy stimulates your O-Spot."

"Moving on," she continued, "Men who do not finish their thrust as deep in a woman as they can do not know what they are doing. Stimulating a woman's O-spot is a major source of pleasure, so is her Hot Spot and the only way to do both is a deep thrust."

"Now some women find Cervical contact to be uncomfortable or painful. Not to put too fine a point on it, this is another example of men not knowing what they are doing."

"We teach men to make the first thrust very slowly. The key is slow and gentle. If this is done too fast Cervical contact can hurt, sometimes a lot, but slow and gentle is delightful. If you've had a lot of good foreplay, and your guy's first thrust is decadently slow, a deep full thrust and full Cervical stimulation never hurts and can be one of the most enjoyable parts of sex. Women miss out on a vast amount of pleasure because men don't know the value of really slow thrusts.

"The next thing to understand is that these nerve endings take a bit of time to react to stimulus, so this is another reason why all of a man's thrusts should be slow as well as deep. When his Hilt is in contact with your Hot Spot, he should pause for a second This is how a man maximizes a woman's pleasure. After the first thrust, the one that gently stretches her out, the rest are not as slow as his first, but still slow."

She looked at me and smiled. I had thought I knew a lot, and just found out I didn't know very much at all. I would have been a little embarrassed, but she did not make a point of rubbing it in.

She looked at me and smiled again, "Around here, all of our guys are going have the basic decency to do really good foreplay with you for a long time. Frankly, anything less is just selfishly rude. When it's time to enter you, they will make sure your legs are spread wide and thrust into you with a delicious slowness; they will finish as deep in you as they can get, pause for a second when they get there, and you will feel each thrust in the center of your soul."

"*Wow*," I thought to myself, but said nothing.

"The part of a guy's anatomy directly above his Cock is called his Hilt, and finishing a deep thrust brings it into contact with your Labia where he can use it to stimulate your Hot Spot. The best way to do this is for him to make a little hip roll up which you meet with a little hip roll down. With his Cock fully in your Pussy, and this combination of hip rolls your Hot Spot gets better stimulated than it can any other way. No girl can do with her finger anything nearly as nice as what the two of you can do together with his Cock in your Pussy. When you are with a guy who really knows what he's doing, a finger or a sex toy is a very poor substitute for a hard hot Cock."

As she nodded, I thought about all the times I'd had to rub my Hot Spot while having sex.

"So," I interrupted, "You're saying we should not have to finger ourselves while having sex?"

She smiled, "With a guy who knows what he's doing, never, not ever, no matter what. That is the guy's job and all he has to do is to go really deep and roll over your Hot Spot with his Hilt. In this way, all four of your orgasmic zones are stimulated with each thrust. We call this a "Full Sensation Thrust," but you'll learn a lot more about this later today." She looked at me, smiled and winked.

"Now there is something wonderful that happens for a woman when they share excellent foreplay, and your partner has all four of your orgasmic zones firing at the same time. It takes your orgasm to a level beyond imagination. We call this an Epicurean Experience. The orgasm part itself is called a Whole Body Orgasm because it resonates through your whole body in waves. Just so you know, it is more intense than anything you've ever experienced, its often accompanied by squirting or female ejaculation, which happens often enough with us that we gave this its own name… Squirts. It'll happen a lot so unless you like sleeping on wet sheets, you ought to use a towel. A full Epicurean has three parts, excellent foreplay, a four level orgasm brought on by Full Sensation Thrusting, and a third part."

"Now, eventually your guy is going to have his orgasm. One of the great things about Full Sensation Thrusts is it will take a nice long time for him to get there.

When your guy has his orgasm, he thrusts into you completely and holds his Hilt against your Hot Spot. You feel each and every one of his orgasmic thrusts resonate through your whole body as he pumps his nice hot cum as deep into as it can get. The pleasure brought on by feeling his orgasm and the wonderful warmth of his cum is the third part of an Epicurean Experience."

"After that, the next thing that happens around here is simple enough. You and your partner let everything calm down, and just stay together. You Epicurean comes down from the peaks to a lower level we call an Afterglow Orgasm which a man truly committed to your pleasure can keep going for a long time. This is how a guy relishes the incomparable luxury of tender intimacy with you."

"You can't possibly imagine what the totality of an Epicurean Experience feels like and then followed up by an Afterglow Orgasm, but you won't have to for long. You'll have several a little later today and then you'll know."

She smiled at me warmly. "A girl's first Epicurean changes us, Mary Ellyn. It changed me, and it'll change you too. The first thing is this, it changes your perspective on men. You learn just how much pleasure they can actually bring you and it's more than you ever imagined. Once this happens, what we hope for from a man is never the same. It turns us all from passive followers, letting him just do his thing to us and hoping we get our share, into women who ask for what we want and show them how when they don't know. Once we've had an Epicurean or two, we know what we want and no longer accept second rate."

"So, moving on," she continued, "I doubt that any man has ever actually made love with you. Not the way we define it here." She looked at the question in my eyes and continued, "First, most women describe making love as... Great Sex... but for us 'making love' is more than that; It is "making *Eros* love," and this requires an emotional connection between both partners first. Making *Eros* love does not happen without a strong emotional connection."

I held up my hand to ask a question. "Ever since my conversation with Helena, I've wondered how that happens with people who hardly know each other? I mean, I don't really have strong emotional connections with guys I know fairly well."

"That's a good question, Mary Ellyn. This connection is found through excellent foreplay."

"Foreplay?" I asked.

Debbie chuckled and shook her head negatively, "No, child, not just 'foreplay,' it's 'Excellent' foreplay. 'Excellence' is the key. You'll see for yourself soon enough." She nodded with a smile. "When a man is doing excellent foreplay, he is slowly... savoring... you, taking his time, drinking in the wonderful essence of your femininity... like the fine wine Helena mentioned. Meanwhile you are doing the same with him, savoring him, drinking in his marvelous masculine essence like a fine wine. Two people who do this together form a very strong emotional connection in a short time even if they hardly know each other. This happens with excellent foreplay."

I nodded. So, this is what Helena had been talking about.

After a moment, Debbie continued. "During the first few days, this is what is going to happen. We will be pairing you up with a series of men, priests here at the resort, who are going to 'make *Eros* love' with you. They are going to rock your world. Plus you are going to go out on the resort and enjoy both the amenities, and the guests who are out there."

Next, she brought out a small wooden box with oriental markings. "These," she explained, "are Ben Wah Balls. You insert them into your Pussy before your daily martial arts session." She smiled, "They work like Kagel exercises, only better. To start with, just use one, eventually you'll work up to three or four. These keep your Vaginal muscles toned. You're going to be making *Eros* love a lot, and over time this tends to loosen things. You need to keep those muscles toned, just like your other muscles."

I looked at the stainless steel balls in the box. They were about the size of medium size marbles. "So, this is how a girl screws a lot and still keeps her Pussy tight?"

"Yes," Debbie answered with a pleasant chuckle, "Anyway, you can use the Ben Wah Balls pretty much anytime you're not with a guy, but our priestesses find it works well to use them during your martial arts session.

"Martial arts?" I asked.

"Tae Kwon Do," she answered. "You'll take a class everyday but Sunday. You'll find it empowering."

"Really? How?" I asked.

"First of all, Martial Arts are great for building confidence," she began. "We don't face a lot of threats around here, but that really isn't the main thing about Tae

Kwon Do. Confidence is. The confidence becomes a part of who you are."

"I see," I smiled.

"And then there is the idea that whenever we say 'no' it does not mean 'no' but 'hell no.'" She looked at me with a serious expression.

"OK," I answered. I liked that idea, a lot. "But what do we say 'no' to around here?"

"Lots of things," she parsed her lips and looked at me, "BDSM, never, not ever, no matter what. Things like blow jobs, and rough sex too. None of these things honor Aphrodite. They are about a guy using us for his pleasure with little regard for ours. Yes, we can have some fun like that, but not as an equal. *Eros* love is always about two people coming together as equals."

She paused, "Enough about that. It's time to get you ready. Here," Debbie said handing me a little red dress, and matching high heels with a knowing smile on her face. She looked at her watch. "Put these on. Your first guy's name is Thomas. He is going to start introducing you to Aphrodite."

Now, let me tell you something about the little red dress. This has nothing to do with color. It has to do with length. Women measure short dresses from the knee up. Men measure them from the Pussy down. Eight inches down is a nice suggestion of what may become available to some lucky guy. Six is a woman's equivalent of a walking wolf whistle. Four is a strong suggestion of what is likely to become available, and sorry girls, but two or three verges on begging for it.

The LRD that Debbie gave me would have to be stretched some to get to three inches down. As if this were not enough, the sides were slit above my hips, allowing the ties of the thong panties to be clearly visible. The cleavage was cut down almost to my belly button with the back equally low. The strapless bodice draped loosely over my breasts which meant they could be effortlessly exposed, and the dress would come off altogether with a simple tug over my head.

Not only that, Debie provided no panties.

I rolled my eyes in an unspoken question.

Debbie just smiled. "You're going to have a lot of fun today, Mary Ellyn; oh yes, you certainly are."

"Commando?" I asked. I'd never had the courage to do this in a really short skirt before. "In a dress this short? What if he… "

"What if he sees your Pussy?" Debbie laughed out loud, "Girl, he is going to see all of you and do a whole lot more than just look."

She smiled and intentionally softened her tone, "Look, I know you have a lot to get used to, and it's normal to be insecure at first, but every girl should be as sexy as the social circumstances let her get away with. Here in the Bay, you have few limits. You need to wear a dress to the restaurants, but we all put on a show."

"Thongs are sexy but can also be really uncomfortable. Plus, I absolutely hate wedgies, don't you? Commando is even sexier than a thong, especially if you find a way to let the guy know, plus you're always comfortable, and it makes you feel free. With those slits on the sides, he'll know you're commando, and that is what you want."

She looked at me for a minute. "Most of Aphrodite's priestesses have little use for panties, even when wearing really short skirts. We love to find ways to get guys excited because they love it so. There are so many things we want them to do for us, so we need to do everything we can for them. Creating a high level of anticipation is a wonderful thing for a woman to do for a man we know is going to score. Most of us find a way to give him a flash of what we're not wearing because prick teasing is delightful fun for both of you. Guys love being teased like this. Especially here. Do you know why?"

"No," I answered honestly.

"Because they know the tease includes a promise," she answered just as honestly, "One you're going to keep."

"*Hmmmm*," I thought to myself, not for the last time.

"This is going to be great fun, so show off a little, it's good for you," Debbie concluded with a nod and a smile.

I met Thomas for lunch in front of the Crystal Martini. He was dressed in nice Bermuda shorts and a flowered shirt and he suggested we go to the bar. As we were settling into the bar stools, he noticed me trying to sit without revealing too much… hard to do when you are commando in a dress that comes down three inches from your Pussy. I did not succeed very well, and he got a good look.

Here's the thing, I knew he saw everything, but he was so suave about it. No leering look, no embarrassing comments, just class. The exact way a guy ought to behave.

"Mary Ellyn," he asked nonchalantly as if nothing of significance had occurred. "May I order you a drink?"

I smiled and set about regaining my composure. "Yes," I replied, "I'll have a Hendrick's Martini, dry, up, with three cocktail onions." I know a lot of people don't consider that a woman's drink, but I don't care about those things. A properly prepared martini tastes like an ice-cold cloud, and I like what I like. Anyone who doesn't like it can go pound sand.

"Oh, that sounds good," he agreed with a smile and a nod. "I'll have one too." He ordered our drinks and went right on to getting menus and discussing lunch options as if nothing unusual had happened. The flash of Pussy was nothing other than pleasant eye candy, nothing more remarkable than showing cleavage.

Now that was cool. This man was completely comfortable around women. I found I was completely comfortable around him. I wondered if the two were connected. "*Hmmmm.*"

I decided to do what Debbie suggested and show off. It was easy. In that dress, all I had to do was stretch a little, which I did now and then.

We ate at the bar. I had this marvelous crawfish étouffée for lunch. After lunch, Thomas leaned over and suggestively kissed me. "Would you like to go back to your bungalow?"

"Yes," I answered and got off of the barstool. There was no way to do this without giving him a nice look, so I just went with it and showed off. Given what Debbie said was about to happen, there was no point in being shy.

When we reached my bungalow and went in, I half expected to move directly to sex, but this did not happen. Instead, he gently led me to the couch, and we just sat down. He began asking me how I liked the resort. Dressed like I was this was astonishing. An LRD like I was wearing has one purpose, and that is to demand male attention on female anatomy. But Thomas was talking to me almost as if I were in a sweatshirt and jeans or something. Now that was really cool.

I had to admit, waiting was enticing, but finally Thomas reached over and stroked my cheek gently and kissed me lightly with an inviting open mouthed kiss. *Great kiss,* I thought to myself as we made out like this for a few minutes. Then he ran his hand down and exposed my breasts and began fondling my nipples as we kissed. Once in a while, he'd put his hand between my legs and take the middle finger and gently run it from the top of my groove slowly, gently to the bottom, but just once, and then bring it back up to my nipple. Everything was slow, everything gentle. My anticipation was off the charts.

After a while, he stood and extended me his hand and led me back to the bedroom. The room had a free-standing full-length mirror, and I could see myself as we walked in. With my breasts exposed, the vision was stunning... to him. You could tell by the look on his face as he looked at me in the mirror. This was a man who was highly experienced with beautiful girls, yet he found me stunning. The look on his face could not be a lie. He spoke no words, but the message was clear. But I'm not stunning. Very nice, yes, but not stunning, not to a man experienced with beautiful girls, and then it hit me. He was stunned by femininity in general. This was a man who loved women, and all of us could do this to him. *Hmmmm,* I thought to myself again.

Once we were beside the bed, he pulled me to him and began kissing me, rather softly considering the way I was dressed. He moved his hand to the middle of my back and began to rub me from the middle slowly down to the crack of my ass.

Then he looked into my eyes. "Control, Mary Ellyn, is one of the most important forms of strength a man can have. Without this he will never be a great lover."

"So, you aren't going to ravish me?" I asked. "I've always thought that was the point of a dress like this."

"No," he answered. "Love is to be savored, not rushed, no matter how you are dressed... even if you aren't dressed at all." He chuckled pleasantly, "Especially if you are not dressed at all."

"Are you a great lover?" I asked.

He didn't answer, just smiled, kissed me, and took the hem and slowly, seductively pulled the dress up over my head. All I had left were my shoes, but shoes don't count. I did the natural thing for a girl in this position, slid into his embrace, placed one of his hands on my breast, the other on my ass, and kissed him back. I spread my legs apart and moved his thigh between them. I started to rub my Pussy up and down his pants and learned a really neat lesson. It's deliciously fun to be standing with a fully clothed guy and tease him while you are completely naked. It drives him crazy in a really fun way for both partners.

"Would you like to unbutton my shirt?" he asked.

I nodded. I enjoyed undressing a man as much as any man could possibly enjoy undressing me. I unbuttoned his shirt and removed it. I could not resist running my fingers through is chest hair, feeling the firm musculature underneath.

"My pants?" he asked.

I unclasped his belt, undid the button, unzipped the zipper, and dropped his shorts. He was commando underneath. Almost involuntarily, I kneeled and licked the body of his Cock several times, then drew the head slowly into and then out of my mouth. I kissed the head as I stood back up. He pulled me against him and let me feel his erection in my Venus Mons, then he placed his Cock between my legs, put his hands on my ass and just held me close as he kissed me, using the body of his Cock to massage my groove.

We stood together like this for several delightful minutes. I could feel the body of his Cock press into my groove, and his Hilt press into my Venus Mons as he massaged my ass. My nipples were being tantalizingly teased by his chest hair. His kisses were divine. This was foreplay on a level I had never before experienced, did not know existed. I drank him in, and drank him in, and drank him in some more. It was intoxicating, and I realized this was what he was doing with me. For the first time in my life a man was taking the time to savor me, and I was savoring him.

"*Glorious*," I thought. "Would you like to lie down?" he suggested.

I nodded and we lay down next to each other. He began kissing me softly again and taking my nipple and gently massaging it with his fingers. I could feel the longing ache in my other nipple, and tug of desire building in my Pussy. Then he began a combination of suckling one nipple and nibbling the other and the wave of sensation between my breasts and my Pussy rose to a crescendo.

While he suckled and nibbled my breast, he moved his other hand down, placed his middle finger in my Venus Mons and slowly ran it down to the Intro, gathered moisture there and distributed it upwards several times. He began delicately stroking my Hot Spot while nibbling my nipple.

Then he stopped nibbling and looked into my eyes. At the same time, he placed his middle finger at my Intro, inserted it, and found my G-spot.

I moaned.

He stroked it gently.

I moaned louder. What else can a girl do?

"Thomas," I begged, as he continued to massage my G-spot, and all the while he maintained eye contact in between his soft sensuous kisses. I had never been this enraptured with a man in my life, and we were not even to the main event yet.

He got up and kneeled between my legs, spreading them wide. He placed his Cock into my Intro. He moved it in and out a little several times and then began to fill me. The thickness of his Cock opened me slowly, and I felt his wonderful thick warmness move up my Pussy as he completely filled me with one deliberately slow thrust and he finished with an upward roll across my Hot Spot. I rotated my hips against his final drive in my own counter roll like Debbie had mentioned and we paused at the end, holding nice light pressure against my Hot Spot. The pleasure was intense as we paused, and I moaned loudly in ecstasy.

Dear God in Heaven, that was nice. I must admit, I'd not understood what Debbie meant by "decadently slow," or that I would feel him in the "center of my soul." Those were pleasant sounding ideas but held no real meaning. But now I knew exactly what she meant and as great as I had thought they sounded; the reality was better.

He pulled almost all of the way out, letting the Head of his Cock nestle for a second, and then slowly opened me. This time for the first time, I began to understand what the slowness really meant. I could feel the thickness and the warmness of his Cock, the wonderful wetness of Aphrodite's Nectar as he opened me.

These sensations weren't lost in the speed and felt so nice when you had the time to feel them. Then these sensations moved up and slowly across my G-spot and I felt it more fully than ever before, this thick wet warmness got to my Cervix and touched me gently, and I felt the full thick warmness of him as he filled me and stretched my Pussy out, felt his Hilt press into my Hot Spot, and the wonderful sensations as he paused. In that pause, I could feel everything come to completion, and I have loved a guy being slow from that minute until now. Every sensation is stronger, richer, more glorious and the delightful slowness allows you to enjoy them far more fully. I moaned louder. He did it yet again and I had tears running down my face.

After his next thrust I started pounding the bed with my hands, and I knew why Fantasy Bay called these Full Sensation Thrusts.

This way of firing all four of my orgasmic zones simultaneously was way better than Debbie advertised. Thomas kept on pulling all the way out, then thrusting slowly all the way in again, and we finished his thrusts with our hip rolls together over and over, and I was having an orgasm like none before, beyond anything I could have imagined. I did not feel connected to the earth, or any earthly reality. All I could feel was him, his Cock, his warmth, his thickness, but in a more complete way than I'd ever felt a man before.

"So this is an Epicurean Experience!" I thought to myself, and then remembered, this was still the first part, the last was yet to come.

Women lose all track of time and place when in the embrace of a great lover. I have no idea how long Thomas kept this going, but after a good long time I felt his orgasm gathering and he started to moan too. Right before his orgasm began, Thomas slowly thrust all of his Cock into me and then stopped and held pressure against my Hot Spot with his Hilt. I felt every single one of his hard, short, orgasmic thrusts in a new way. Each was connected to me and resonated with a wonderful warmth through my entire body, one after the next, after another until he was complete. Along the way I felt the heat of his cum explode in my depths which seemed to bring on Squirts and I moaned in tearful unbridled ecstasy.

I had never been that well connected to a man's orgasm. I had no idea that a woman could be. I have always enjoyed the warn sensation of a guys cum as it explodes into me, but other than that, I'd always thought my orgasm was mine and his was his, but this is not true, at least not for women. But I know now, and my first Epicurean Experience was so far beyond spectacular, words fail.

Once his orgasm was complete, Thomas did not pull out right away, and I was glad for the towel, because I'd had Squirts. We just lay there with him completely filling me until our breathing returned to normal, and then stayed together, moving softly, and sharing the hip rolls now and then. My orgasm receded from its peak but continued gently in an Afterglow Orgasm that was softer, fuller, wonderful in a different way. A guy's Cock completely filling your Pussy, but not moving in and out much, just filling you with his warm thickness, small tender motions and gentle intimacy. This creates its own set of precious sensations, not nearly as intense but altogether as wonderful.

Thomas kept our Afterglow Orgasm going for about thirty minutes… after… his orgasm, relishing the oneness of *Eros* with me. After he left, I lay there in my bed luxuriating for a few minutes. I remembered Helena's words and knew it was all true.

"A guy starting things by taking the time to slowly savor the essence of my femininity as if it were a fine wine to be leisurely cherished… caring enough for my pleasure to move slowly enough, deeply enough, that I felt his every thrust through to the center of my soul… to finish by staying in me and taking the time to gently relish the incomparable luxury of tender intimacy with me.

I'd heard the words, but this had happened to me now. All of it. I had been in the arms of a guy who did this with me, and the level of joy I'd felt was even better than I'd thought it would be. Helena's words were as alive with meaning for me now as they had been for her. I just lay there happily until I heard Debbie knocking at the door. I threw on a robe and let her in.

She took one look at me. "Well, I see you and Thomas got along well."

I was kind of speechless.

"It's written all over your face, child," she explained. "You're still flushed."

"You have no idea," I replied with a broad smile.

"Oh, yes I do." Debbie laughed, and blew me a kiss. "I've been there a thousand times, and each time it's always like the first time. Epicureans never get old."

She walked into the Bedroom, unzipped one of the suitcases there, and began hanging up negligees. For those first few days, Debbie was the one who picked out clothes for me. I didn't see how I was going to learn much from this, but I was wrong. Really wrong. Debbie had me in a red see through camisole that high-lighted my long blonde hair, with red, tie-on, translucent bra and panties, a red garter belt, and red fishnets. "Not all girls should wear red," she said, as she looked me over, "but you do it very nicely. It goes with your skin tones. Go, have a look." She pointed at the wall mirror.

Wow, I thought as I stood looking at myself in the full length mirror.

"Here," Debbie said handing me several men's magazines. "Open the top one to the centerfold," she suggested.

I did as she asked and looked at the pictures there.

"Now," she continued, "I want you to show me the features the girl in the picture has that are better than what you have."

I stood there looking back and forth from the pictures to the mirror.

"Well, the cat's got your tongue I see." She laughed. "Here, I'll help you. Let's look at her tits." We looked at the picture for a moment.

"My, oh my," she exclaimed, in mock shock, "yours are a little bigger. Imagine that."

It was true. At this point in my life, my cup size was D. The chick in the picture was certainly gorgeous, but not more than a very nicely airbrushed C.

"Good," Debbie said. "Good. What about her ass? Better than yours? Nope! Legs? Nope! So, tell me what's better about the girl in the magazine than you?"

"Well, she's naked, posed by a pro and airbrushed, and I'm in a negligée, but other than that, there really isn't a lot of difference," I answered slowly as I took the first steps on the journey of understanding myself in a new way.

"Right! Now," Debbie continued. "Other than the fact that you are real, and these centerfolds are just ink on a page, do you know the main difference between these girls and most women?" she asked.

"No," I answered. The truth was, I had no idea.

"Confidence and enthusiasm! These girls are all projecting their sexuality with confidence in their desirability, and enthusiasm about what a man might do with them. They are doing it very well."

I nodded slowly and Debbie continued, "You are beautiful, Mary Ellyn, and the truth is all women either are or can be. Feminine beauty takes many forms, not just what appeals to the Hugh Hefner wantabes of the world. These centerfolds just know they are sexy and put it out there. Beyond that there really is nothing any more special about them than all of the rest of us. We're all special, it's just that most of us don't know it."

She stopped, drew in her breath, exhaled, and went on, "Enthusiasm about what a man might want to do with you and the confidence to project are two of Aphrodite's gifts, but you have to find it in yourself. Once you do, you can put it out there too. These girls are so sexy because they believe they are, and once they believe it, they flaunt it. They accentuate their features, minimize their flaws, and feed on the positive. It is their attitude about themselves and men that makes the difference. No physical feature of any woman is sexier to a man, than an attitude like that."

She pointed at the magazines. "So how did these girls get that way? I will tell you something. They did not pay much attention to the mean things girls say, or the airbrushed pictures in women's magazines. They listened to guys. They view themselves as guys see them. That is where they got the confidence to project it like they do."

"From guys?" I asked in disbelief.

"Yep." Debbie paused again. "Guys!"

Debbie paused again to collect her thoughts. "Aphrodite does not make mistakes, Mary Ellyn. All women are beautiful, maybe not to every guy out there, but to enough that her dreams can come true, and Aphrodite has given each and every woman all over the world... gifts. And these gifts include the right to enjoy them. We all have the divine right to love ourselves, love our sexuality and if a woman is unattached to enjoy sharing Aphrodite's gifts with any unattached man without shame."

I nodded slowly. This way of thinking was a revelation.

Debbie nodded. "That is the main lesson today. You are going to have a lot of fun with men, Mary Ellyn, and they are going to have a lot of fun with you, and you are going to learn things about yourself... and... men you haven't even guessed at yet. These are gifts of Aphrodite, and you have the right to enjoy all of it. Now, Will is going to be here soon, so it's time for me to leave."

"*A divine right to love being a woman, to love our sexuality, and enjoy sharing it without shame!*" I thought to myself as Debbie showed herself out, "*What a profound concept.*"

Chapter Three

Will arrived less than five minutes after Debbie left. As I took his hand and we exchanged the normal greetings, I realized that to call him gorgeous was an understatement. He was tall, with dark hair, dark eyes and a dazzling smile. But more than that, he looked so deeply into my eyes, that all I could see were his eyes. We were sitting on my sofa but all I could see were his deep liquid eyes. We made pleasant small talk for a few minutes, and then he stood and offered me his hand. He led me back to the bedroom and once there, he stroked my face and kissed me lightly. After a few minutes, he unfastened the ties at the top of my Baby Doll and let it fall around my ankles, untied my bra, and it joined the baby doll on the floor; then encircled my waist with his hands and gently pulled me to him.

He began kissing me while massaging my back with his hands. There was nothing hurried or rushed about this. As he massaged my back, I removed his G-String. After Thomas and now Will, I was learning that slow is a luxurious gift for a man to give a woman. It has to be hard for a guy. You're naked in his arms and his every instinct is to move things along. Instead, he paces himself, moves forward slowly, here a little, there a little, taking his time and this is so good for making *Eros* love.

Will was... savoring... me. He was drinking in my femininity and loving the flavor. The physical sensations he created with his foreplay were terrific, but the emotional reaction in my soul was over the top. Being slowly savored by a guy is a true joy for a girl. It validates everything about your femininity. And the other thing was, I got to have the time to drink him in, and girls, this drink is the best adult beverage in the world.

After a little while, we lay down, and Will continued kissing me, but not French Kissing. Will's kiss was different, better, a sensuous soft caress of my lips with his and an occasional tongue tickle. Then he'd pull away and look into my eyes. Then his lips would lightly touch mine again, and he would pull away and look deeply into my eyes. It was as if he were caressing my eyes with his.

I caught on and went with the flow, and we just kissed like this for a while. A luscious lip caress followed by a rapt gaze into each other's eyes… the most sensuous kissing I had ever done, beyond any I had ever dreamed could be done. The neatest thing was, it was not just him doing this with me, I was doing it with him too. It was natural and intoxicating.

Then, he began softly touching me with his fingers… but not my erogenous zones. While softly kissing my lips, and then gazing into my eyes, Will began gently caressing my face, my neck, my shoulders. After a little while, he ran a finger between my cleavage, down almost to the top of my Venus Mons, then back up and traced the bottom edge of my breasts a few times but he never massaged them or touched my nipples, all while alternating between caressing me with his eyes, then his lips. He moved his hand to my garter belt and traced around to one of the garters, followed that down to the fishnets, and traced the top around to the inside of my thigh, moving slowly and softly. He stroked the top seam cf the stocking a number of times.

Then his fingers went up the inside of my thigh to the seam of my panties, and again, slowly and gently traced their bottom seam in the vicinity of my Pussy, but never actually touching me there. By the time he'd done this several times, I wanted him in me so badly I was about to cry, and yet my tits were unfondled, and my panties were still on. Who knew a guy could do this to you so easily? I didn't.

We kissed and gazed into each other's eyes and kissed again while he touched with me gently for what seemed like an hour… in the vicinity of my erogenous zones, but without actually touching any of them. This type of foreplay was more sensual than my imagination had ever dared to explore. Frankly, who would have ever thought of it? Finally, it became more than I could bear, and I began to beg. I couldn't help it.

"Please," I said softly. He didn't seem to hear me.

"Will, please," I repeated a little louder as he stroked the seam of my panties. His only response was to move his hand from stroking the seam of my panties on one side, across my Pussy to the seams on the other side. So frustratingly nice. What do you do when you absolutely, positively have to have a man's Cock in you and he won't?

"Please, Will, please," I pleaded, "I need you," I had tears forming in my eyes.

He smiled, kissed my tears away and then looked back into my eyes. "That's what I was waiting for." He rose up, kneeled between my legs, spreading them, and began untying my panties, and sensuously removing them. I had never known a guy being so slow could be so frustratingly wonderful. I watched the look in Will's eyes as he undressed me, and for the first time began to understand everything Debbie had been saying. Will was looking at me with what could only be described as relish. I had never watched a man's face as he looked at me naked before. No one had ever given me the time. The look in those eyes was a revelation. The looks that play across a man's face in the process of him slowly stripping and gently playing with you add a wonderful dimension to foreplay for a woman.

I had thought my pleading would hurry him up, but it did not. This wonderful man was not in a hurry. My begging moved us to the next phase, but he was delightfully, deliciously, nearly maddingly slow. It was obvious he liked looking at me naked, playing with me naked. It became obvious he wanted me to luxuriate in his every move, so I did the only thing I could; I relaxed, surrendered to his touch and just soaked him in and moaned.

Finally, he used his Cock to rub my Hot Spot for a while, then finally slid it down into my Intro. He let it sit there for a few seconds. Then with one slow firm motion of his Cock, he entered and opened me. The slowness allowed me to feel his thick warmness and my wetness and created a wave of pleasure. Then he slowly filled me passing my G-spot, creating another wave. His thick warm wetness continued to fill me until his Cock got to my Cervix, creating yet another wave as he slowly stretched my Pussy out to the full depth of his Cock and finished with a final firm drive as far into me as a Cock could go with an upward move of his Hilt firmly across my Hot Spot. I met his finishing roll with my counter roll, and the two together set off another wave that resonated with the first three, and I screamed in an unbridled joy that was worth the wait.

At that moment, I loved being a woman more than I ever had before.

Everything Will did with me was slow and deliberate. After that first deep thrust, he pulled about a third of the way out and slowly thrust all the way back into me, stretching me out fully, and connecting his Hilt with my Hot Spot again. He repeated this shorter stroke two or three more times, then he slowly drew his Cock almost all of the way out, so that it just nestled there in the Intro. He paused for a second. It was almost like he hit a reset button.

Then started back in slowly again. His delightfully warm Cock eased my Intro open, setting off the first wave of pleasure, passed my G-spot slowly enough so I could feel it there, continued to my Cervix and all the way back in until his Cock almost completely filled me, and then he drove the Hilt of his Cock home. He paused there for a few seconds, made three or four shorter strokes, each time he filled me completely, finishing with a thrust / counterthrust… all the while caressing me with his lips and his eyes. Soft, slow and delicious with a firm finish. It almost sounds like a fine wine, doesn't it. No wine I've ever heard of was as nice as making *Eros* love with Will.

Let me tell you about his eyes. It was like looking into infinity. His eyes were caressing me in a way I had never been touched before. I had never imagined that this sort of eye contact could draw you into your partner's soul, but I cannot come up with a better explanation of what was happening. His eyes drew me into him, and they also told their own wordless story. This man wanted me. Not just his Cock in my Pussy, but me. All of me. He thought I was worth all of the time he could manage to take so he could savor me. No one had ever paid me a compliment like this before.

It seemed like our bodies melded into one. He drew me into him with his eyes. There were no boundaries between us. For the second time in my life, I was truly one with a man.

Have you ever heard girls use the term "transported?" I had, several times, and had always thought the girls were just gaga, but as Will and I became one, we were "transported." I wasn't sure where we were, but it didn't feel like this world. Not heaven either exactly, maybe some other place in between. It would be some time before I fully realized what was happening, or where we were, but I loved it there After another well connected orgasm we just lay there together. I have no idea how long. We were some place near heaven and neither of us had any interest in leaving. I learned many things from Will that day. I had no idea a man's eyes could be such a part of making *Eros* love. I had no concept of how wonderful slow sensuous foreplay could be or that it did not have to involve a woman's erogenous zones directly. I had no idea a man could thrust into me slowly enough to create four distinct waves of pleasure, or how high a girl would get when a guy made *Eros* love like this with you.

As wonderful as Thomas was, he turned out to have been the appetizer, Will was the main course. You might think all of this would have been enough for my first day, but that's not the way things work at Fantasy Bay. Debbie gave me a pair of high heels designed for the pool and taught me how to walk... well... perhaps "saunter" is a better word.

All girls wiggle our ass when we walk. It's part of our hip structure, not really something we practice once we've outgrown preteen sleepovers. But there is a difference between walking like a girl and sauntering like a priestess. Why do we put such an emphasis on women being what men want? Why would we 'saunter,' for example? Isn't this just yielding to misogyny? No... not if you expect men to be all they can be for you! The world of Aphrodite is governed by the idea that each gender is going to be all they can be for the other.

The first part of sauntering is really simple. You hold your shoulders back and keep your tummy tucked. This thrusts your breasts out and shows them off.

The next thing you do is swing your legs wide so when you put your foot down, your feet are about two feet apart. This shows off the space between your legs, even when you are wearing a miniskirt. Men... love... being reminded about the space between a woman's legs. When you put this all together, you don't exactly walk, you saunter.

This is the way the priestesses of Aphrodite walk. We love being women, we love showing off, we love being all we can be for men. For us, projecting our sexuality is like a Christian wearing a cross. So, was that enough for Debbie on day one? Nope.

"Nude?" I asked incredulously, standing there in a hat, high heels, sunglasses, and nothing else. "I'm going out to the pool like this? Naked?"

"Not quite," Debbie answered with a laugh, handing me a beach towel. "When you get to the Tiki Bar, go up to a waitress, and she will hand you a white mesh coverup."

"Oh," I answered. "OK, and then what?"

"You put on the coverup, and then walk out and around the pool deck," she began. "Go toward the deeper end; that's the right side. The guys around the pool are not instructors," she continued, "they are regular guests. The looks you get from those men will build a lot of confidence, Mary Ellyn. I know you believed the looks you got from Will and Thomas. Believe what the looks you'll get around the pool tell you too. Pay attention to their reaction… to you. Confidence and enthusiasm about men whenever you're around men makes everything work well for a woman. Without it, almost nothing works very well. You are going to be afraid. Fear is a killer. If you can defeat the fear of being practically naked in front of men you don't know, you can defeat the fear of anything in life you might ever face."

"OK," I replied as I nodded slowly. "But what if they want to… am I allowed to…"

"Oh, yes." She nodded again with a broad smile. "They… will… want to Mary Ellyn. Every single guy around that pool is going to want to make *Eros* love with you. And you… are… allowed to."

She paused and looked at me. "The men here need to build confidence with women just like you need to build confidence with them. We teach these men to be classy and confident, but just like you, they have to practice it. If you like the way a man approaches you, Mary Ellyn, say yes, and have some fun. If you don't, say no. It won't be long 'till someone else comes up."

So, I practiced sauntering, wrapped in a beach towel, over to the closest Tiki Bar and walked up to a waitress. She smiled when she saw me wrapped in my towel and wordlessly reached under the counter and got out a "coverup."

Debbie lied.

That's all I can tell you.

She did! The bitch lied.

There was no "cover" to the "coverup."

The mesh was thin string, and the strings were an inch apart. A half inch hem formed the bottom and came down past my Pussy about three inches. That coverup "covered" nothing. Every guy who saw you was going to see everything. Both of my nipples stuck through the strings, the full arc of my breasts could not be missed, nor my narrow waist, nor hips, and if I sauntered like I'd been taught, my Pussy would be on full display, especially if a guy was sitting down.

I looked around the pool deck; there were about twenty men out there, and all of them were sitting down. If I were pole-dancing totally nude, they would not have a better show.

Then I realized there were some girls around the pool deck too. They were each paired with a guy and were nude too. Completely nude... well... except for a hat and sunglasses, but they don't count, and I could tell the guys with them had no eyes for me or anything but the girl sitting with him. Imagine that: a guy paying attention to a naked girl sitting right next to him! I will tell you one thing: those girls had guts, or maybe it was confidence. Probably both.

"Would you care for a drink, ma'am?" the waitress asked, clearly used to a girl standing there in a coverup that was not covering up anything.

"Yes," I answered, "I'd like Hendricks Martini, dry, up, with three cocktail onions."

OK, I thought to myself, and took a long, slow breath. *Fear is my enemy. I need to channel a centerfold. If they can do this, I can do this. Aphrodite has given me gifts and I can put on a show. If that inspires a man to want to screw my brains out, so much the better.*

The waitress delivered my drink, I took a sip, and it was very well done. "*OK.*" I finally decided.

I walked out onto the pool deck with my drink, doing my best to saunter like Debbie had taught me. As I walked past the Bar, and started around the pool, I admit I was nervous. For the first time in my life, I was basically naked in public. There was nowhere to hide the fact there was nothing hidden. Sauntering in a coverup like I was wearing, was truly flaunting it, but this was a scary thing.

The first time a woman does something like this, she doesn't know how it will work out, and it is normal to be afraid of the unknown. That's the way fear works. If it paralyzes you, and forces you to back down, fear wins. I will admit, I was tempted right then to cut and run.

But if you overcome your fear and forge through; fear loses, and that was Debbie's whole point. If I could defeat the fear of being naked in front of all of these guys, I could defeat the fear of anything… ultimately everything I might ever face. Nothing was going to get harder than this. I cowgirled up and sauntered on.

It was only a matter of a few steps in the sunlight until I realized the eyes of all the unattached men on the pool deck were on me. Every single one. They were not just staring they were practically drooling. Over me.

It was liberating. My confidence soared. Debbie was certainly right about that. Sauntering around that pool for the first time, and the looks I got, is something else I will never forget. No girl would. I had faced fear and had it on the run. It felt good, liberating.

I had sauntered less than twenty feet around the pool when a guy came up to me. He also had a drink in his hand. "Hi, my name is Brady," he said holding out his other hand and taking mine. "We both have drinks, could I get us a snack of some kind?" he asked pleasantly, confidently I noted.

"My name is Mary Ellyn," I replied as confidently as I could. After all, I was naked for all practical purposes. "What do you have in mind?"

"How about some Bang Bang Shrimp?" he suggested.

"Oh, I'd love that," I answered. It was not that I'd suddenly found more confidence, I just love Bang Bang Shrimp.

"I'm at the table right over there," he said indicating a table with an umbrella and a towel in one of the lounge chairs.

"I'll wait for you over there, then," I agreed and sauntered over, noticing the drooling envy of the other men watching me. I was about to sit down when another girl walked out onto the pool deck. She was in a cover up just like mine and immediately became the center of attention.

She walked over to me and smiled. "The waitress told me you're a new priestess in training, so I've watched you a little, and you're doing fine. Now, watch me."

She went a few steps farther and the same situation played out. A guy came over and chatted her up. He pointed to a table, and she walked over and stood there waiting. She looked over at me and winked.

Her man began walking back a few moments later with drinks. When he was about twenty feet away, she reached down, took the bottom hem of her coverup, and seductively pulled it up over her head. Now she was naked… completely naked… just like the other girls around the pool. She sauntered over to him, kissed him lightly, and took one of the drinks from his hand. They walked back to their table hand in hand, and she sat down in his lap.

In my life, I had never seen a prick tease done half so well, and I got the drift of what was going on around the pools of Fantasy Bay.

There were a number of men around the pool. You'd think a bunch of them would rush up to a naked woman, wouldn't you? Well, no. The guys sign in at the Tiki Bar and get a pager, like at a restaurant. When it's their turn the pager goes off. It is one at a time. No male power struggles. Brady had approached me when it was his turn.

I looked back at the bar and noticed Brady was returning with the Bang Bang Shrimp. *Well*, I thought to myself, *I'm nearly naked anyway... so... in for a penny, in for a pound.*

I took ahold of the hem and raised my cover up over my head, slowly, just like the other girl had. With my shoulders back, and my legs spread, I sauntered over to him. Nude. The look on his face completed the changes Debbie had started with the magazines. Brady, a regular guest with no agenda, was stunned. By me. It was hard to believe at first, but it was true, and suddenly I realized I had no fear. It had vanished like a fart in the wind.

OK! I thought to myself. I wrinkled my nose coquettishly and tickled the tip of his tongue with mine. Taking my lead from the other girl, I led Brady back to our table and sat down in his lap. As I sat there naked, I understood I had just prick teased him as well as the other girl had.

It was fun. Sooooo… much fun. Prick teasing men should be an Olympic Sport! Can you imagine the protest howls from the prudes? Can you imagine the TV ratings? LOL.

I pointed my tits straight at him, stretched slowly over, selected a shrimp, dipped it in the cocktail sauce, brought my shoulders back as I brought it to my mouth, and nibbled it slowly.

Gloriously naked, without fear, feeling my inner woman liberated in an entirely new way, powerful on a level I had never contemplated.

I decided to up the ante. I got up, selected a shrimp and dipped it in the sauce. I faced Brady, fully naked except for my hat and straddled my legs across his thighs and sat back down with my legs spread about as wide as a girl's legs go. I cannot imagine how a girl flaunts her sexuality any more than this. Brady's mouth fell open. Unabashed, I fed him the shrimp. In the process, I dribbled some sauce onto in chest. I seductively licked it off and took a gentle nibble on his nipple.

He took a shrimp and actually rubbed some of the sauce on my nipple and nibbled it off before feeding me the shrimp.

We alternated nibbling sauce off of each other's nipples and feeding each other shrimp until they were gone. That girls is a podium finish in a prick teasing contest for sure, and I will tell you something. It was fun, and I came away with a higher level of confidence in my sexuality.

Somehow, Brady seemed to understand. This was not just a tease, but also a promise. It showed on his face. Somehow, in the presence of a naked girl in a perfect pose, he held his composure and kept his cool.

I recalled what Thomas said about control. This must be how guys learn this. Brady knew exactly what I was saying without words. "Patience, boy, enjoy the show, and I will make sure you enjoy what is coming even more."

I will tell you this. Debbie lied about the "cover" part of the coverup, but everything else she said was true. Any shortcomings I thought I had were nothing more than figments of my imagination. Screw the unrealistic magazines and mean girls, I believe the guys. When we were finished feeding the shrimp to each other, Brady looked at me. "Would you like to go back to one of the pavilions."

I agreed, and he took me by the hand and led me to a pavilion on the back perimeter. I hadn't realized it, but these pavilions surrounding the pools had double lounges and ceiling fans going. Perfect for making love.

I shook out my long hair, slid into his arms, wrapped a leg around his ass and rested it on the lounge, took his hand and encouraged him to run his fingers through my hair.

Brady and I made out like this for a few moments, then he removed his G-string, lay me down on the lounge, and caressed my breasts.

He ran his finger softly down my groove, slowly from the top to the bottom, making no attempt to go beyond the surface until he got to my Intro. He slowly softly penetrated me enough there to pick up some moisture and moved it up to my Hot Spot. He stroked me like this four or five times, then he settled his finger just above it.

After a brief pause, he began massaging my Hot Spot, gently, slowly, tantalizingly. All the while he kissed me softly. No ravishing. No banging. Someone had taught him well. We had the emotional connection, and I knew that soon we would be making *Eros* love. Brady was a man I hardly knew, yet we were not having sex, we were sharing real love, *Eros* love. Then he began French Kissing me and moved his finger to my Intro, pushed it into me and found my G spot. Thankfully, he entered me not long afterwards, and the sensations of his Cock's thick warmness slowly filling me completely took over my world. Brady was slow, deliberate, and altogether delightful. When it became his time, we had a lovely orgasm together, but mine was a lot longer than his.

Aphrodite has it right, girls. Men may be physically stronger than we are, but I wouldn't change places for anything. I love being a woman. I love what I can do with a man, and more than anything, I was coming to understand and love what a man could do with me.

Chapter Four

Juan smiled to himself and looked at the bungalow address he was headed to. He was softly humming one of his favorite songs.

He loved the sentiments of music. For him, the lyrics of some songs connected him with femininity far better than he could ever find a way to express with words. "Mary Ellyn Cartwright," he said softly reviewing her bio info as he walked. He loved being an instructor at Fantasy Bay. He was well acquainted with the fact that all fine relationships worked well in four areas, the couple's economic model, the social, the emotional, and the physical.

At Fantasy Bay, most of the focus was on the physical and the emotional as the power released by feeding those two areas advanced the couple in the other two.

Juan knew there would come a time when he would want to take up with one of these girls, give her his heart, receive hers in return, and build a relationship like the one Savage Garden was singing about in their song. Those days were still off somewhere in the mists of the future.

The present was a girl named Mary Ellyn. The particular session he was doing today was one of his favorites. Miss Cartwright didn't know it yet, but he was going to take her farther into heaven than she had ever been before.

He loved being a man, loved looking at naked girls, and more than that, he loved playing with naked girls, or ones about to become naked. As a boy, he loved playing football, but now, playing with girls was his favorite sport. He smiled in wonder as he thought of the beauty of Aphrodite's creation and continued walking toward Mary Ellyn Cartwright's bungalow.

He knocked on the door and a woman in a luscious little black dress opened it. This woman was clearly Mary Ellyn Cartwright.

As Juan smiled at Mary Ellyn, he became aware that she was about five foot seven inches tall, maybe a buck thirty-five in weight. In other words, no flab, but not too skinny.

Nice.

She had long legs, nice hips, and a narrow waist. Her leg muscles were nicely toned.

Really nice.

He guessed that her bra's cup size was D. Her breasts were firm, her nipples pert.

Extraordinarily nice.

Her eyes were blue and her hair was dark blonde, long, and she had it arranged so some of it cascaded in front of her shoulders and framed her breasts.

Magnificently nice.

Juan noticed all of this while looking at her face, but slowly her sky blue eyes took over, and he found himself lost in them. Once this happened nothing else mattered much.

Exquisitely nice.

If he were a makeup artist, he could have told you her lip gloss and nail polish were a delightful deep pink that worked well with her basic makeup tone, and complemented well with her blusher, and coordinated with her eye makeup. Not only that, but he was sure the pink matched the color of the interior of her Labia. Woman tease men on a variety of levels and he was OK with this. Pussy pink was every guy's favorite color, why not remind him of it?

He thought of the term he'd heard women use from time to time… Signature Color. Well, he knew one thing about that from a strictly male point of view. A woman's true "Signature Color" was the shade of pink that matched the pink of her Pussy. Once a man had gone down on a woman, her wearing that shade would always enthrall him more than any other. He already was sure he knew the color of Mary Ellyn's Pussy from the shade of pink on her nails. If he hadn't already had a hard on, one look at the color of her nail polish, and he would have.

A makeup artist would have been able to tell you that sky blue of her eyes was perfect with the shade of blue eye shadow, which matched the eye liner, which was deep blue, as was the mascara, and the whole of the marvelously feminine picture was a lot more than the sum of the parts. He knew a thing which most of the good guys all knew. In spite of the glories of a woman's figure, her loveliest feature was her face.

If he were a makeup artist, he could have told you about all of it, but Juan was not a makeup artist. He was a

guy who was going to make *Eros* love with a woman …
this woman… and he was enthralled.

***

Would you think that was all for the first day? Wrong
again. This was easily the best day of my life, but I was
not finished yet.

At about six in the afternoon, Juan knocked on my
door. I opened it, took one look at him and was gaga before
I could help it. This was the best looking guy I had ever
seen in my life. I know we all behold things differently,
and this is a good thing, but for me, this man was the mold
God should make men from.

Juan and I had dinner at the Cuisine L'Europe. I
remembered what the copilot had said about the fresh sole
and ordered Sole Meunière. I'm fond of steak, but fish is
my favorite, and of them all Sole Meunière is the best. The
problem was trying to eat anything around Juan. He was
even better looking than Will. How does a girl act
nonchalant around a guy she can't tear her eyes away
from? If this is a problem for you too, please don't ask me
because after all these years, I still don't know. After a
memorable dinner, we went back to my bungalow.

I thought I'd probably use the red negligée over again,
but Debbie had left me a lot of negligées, so I selected a
light green one instead, and changed into it while Juan
made us Hendrick's Gin Martinis.

I had asked Debbie if the lingerie we used was
normally tie-on. She explained that it was much easier for

either the guy or for us to get them off without breaking the rhythm of the foreplay. She also explained the guy's G-string tied on too, for the same reason.

The "rhythm" of the foreplay. It had never occurred to me that foreplay could have a rhythm to it. What a wonderful concept.

Once I'd finished changing, we sat on my couch and just snuggled for a while.

He kissed me lightly. "How was everything today?"

I drew in a long breath, let it out and answered, "Fine," expecting him to kiss me again. But he didn't.

"How did you like the first guy?" he continued.

It was clear he wanted to talk before we got together. This was new to me... a guy putting a higher priority on talking than screwing. OK, I could adjust to this, it was actually really nice. "He was the best I'd ever had to that point," I answered honestly, "but not my favorite today."

"Now we're getting somewhere." Juan smiled.

He caressed my face. It was clear he was encouraging me to keep talking, so I decided to draw from the liberation I'd felt around the pool, let my barriers down and just open up. I had already beaten fear once today, there was no reason to yield to it now.

I explained how I'd never known what it was to make love with someone, *Eros* love or any other kind. I admitted that no one had ever savored me before and how nice it felt. I explained how I'd never even known what savoring someone while they were savoring me was like until today, or how much better the physical sensations of foreplay were when you took the time to savor each other first. I

73

explained that I never considered foreplay was for anything useful other than to get a girl wet, but I learned from both Thomas and Will, that really good foreplay enhanced everything about making love.

"No one has ever massaged my Venus Mons like he did," I explained. "What a delightful way to slow things down at the same time you're warming them up."

Juan smiled, "It's called a Venus Massage, and it's exactly what you said."

I told him I'd never imagined an Epicurean Experience in my wildest dreams, or experienced a connection to a guy's orgasm before Thomas, but then how truly wonderful it had been with Will, and the way he had caressed me with his eyes and drove me crazy without ever touching my erogenous zones, how he connected me to his orgasm just as well as Thomas, how wonderful it was just lying there with him filling me and moving with each other.

"I've never experienced intimacy that heavenly before," I explained.

"It's called an Afterglow Orgasm," Juan explained, "It's one of my most favorite things." He kissed me softly and encouraged me to continue.

"Good name," I agreed. "I must say, both Thomas and Will seemed to get as much out of it as me, although I was the one having the orgasm."

"They did," Juan replied with a knowing smile and a nod, "For guys it's one of the main benefits of the emotional connection. Through it we are connected to your pleasure and share it with you. A good guy loves the pleasure he creates for you, loves taking the time to create it. It's one of the ways Aphrodite teaches women to use so they can tell good men from the rest."

I nodded, "I'm starting to realize this, but the truth is I never knew it before. I don't think I've ever known a girl who did."

Then we talked about my insecurities walking basically nude around the pool. I talked about the looks on the guys' faces, and how they had made me feel, about the girl who had shown me what I could do, and about the fun I'd had with Brady, first shamelessly prick teasing him, and then the joy of fulfilling everything I'd promised. I finished by kissing Juan lightly and telling him the liberation and power I'd felt around the pool was what helped me open up to him.

"So, you like prick teasing?" He laughed.

"Yes," I answered with a chuckle, "but you know, when we did that to guys in high school and college, a lot of times, we didn't let them score until a lot later, sometimes not at all. That was sort of part of the game."

Juan nodded. "Seems kind of mean, doesn't it?"

"Yes," I agreed and leaned over and kissed him lightly. "But we really weren't all that good at it. Here…"

"You're really good at it?" he asked with a laugh.

"Well… maybe I'm getting better," I answered.

He arched his eyebrows and inclined his head in playful doubt but said nothing.

"OK… yes… I was really good at it today, but it's more than that, I think. Here there is nothing mean. We are actually making a promise… one we're going to follow through on. And you know what," I continued, "the men seem to know this, the looks on their faces were…"

"Priceless?" Juan chuckled.

"Yeah," I agreed. "And I like making promises like that, and then keeping them." I leaned over and tickled his tongue with mine.

"Yes?"—he nodded, raised his eyebrows and smiled—"like the one you just made?"

"Yes." I smiled with a nod.

"Shall we undress?" he asked. I didn't answer, instead, I unbuttoned his shirt, removed it, and I folded it slowly. If the idea was to draw everything out, I could play that game too. Once his shirt was off, I unfastened his belt and unzipped his Bermuda shorts. He stood up and I removed them. I stood and untied his G-string and slipped it off of him. He was spectacularly naked.

"Yes," I agreed coquettishly, "we should undress."

I don't believe any guy had ever slowly, delicately, rhythmically undressed me as a form of foreplay before. Juan massaged my nipples and breasts through my bra and traced out its seams, before removing it. He massaged my Venus Mons, and softly stroked my groove, through my panties, back and forth over and over, taking a full five minutes to remove them. The delicacy with which he touched me and slowly untied the strings and removed my lingerie seemed to be him embracing my femininity and was intoxicating.

Dear God in Heaven, I love it when my lover is drinking in the most essential essence of me. I had no idea there were so many ways a guy could do this.

When Juan was finished undressing me, he moved us on to the next step by asking me to take my tongue and lick his Cock. Then he had me suck it lightly, but made it clear he was not going to come in my mouth.

I truly enjoy playing with a guy's Cock like that but have never particularly enjoyed blow jobs. I will admit that I have never really cared for the taste of cum, but it's more than just that. Even when I was in high school, I loved the feeling of a guy's orgasm in my Pussy, and the feeling of the warmth of his cum inside me. It was never as nice in my mouth. To each her own but I've never been one for blow jobs. I do love playing with a guy's Cock though. I still can't imagine any body parts girls have being as fascinating as a guy's Cock, so I suppose that's why girls do blow jobs. Still rather than see him come with my eyes, and taste his cum in my mouth, I prefer to feel the thick throbbing warmness of his Cock in my Pussy and sense the wonderful warmth of his cum spread inside me.

After a while, the action shifted from Juan to me. He began caressing me and while he began in non-erogenous areas he moved pretty quickly to my nipples and began taking them between his fingers and lightly squeezing them. He kept playing with one breast with his fingers, his massaging action slowly getting stronger. He took my other nipple into his mouth and a commenced a combination of sucking and nibbling. The stronger action with his hand and the nibbling was exciting. I could feel it all the way down to my Pussy. After a bit, he moved his hand down to my Hot Spot and began stroking me lightly while continuing to nibble my nipple.

Then he asked me to assume a doggie position. He opened a drawer on my nightstand. He took out some Vaseline and lubricated my anus. A few seconds later, he thrust his Cock into me there. This was the first time I had ever had anal sex. The boys in high school and college were all about Pussy, not ass.

It was an interesting sensation as he thrust in and pulled out, then thrust in again. It was pleasant, but not the same as vaginal sex. "*The emotional connection enhances everything,*" I thought to myself.

Then he pulled out, turned me over and began to eat Pussy.

This is more like it now, I thought to myself.

He began nuzzling my groove with his nose, then started licking my Hot Spot with his tongue. After a few moments, he inserted a finger into my Pussy and found my G-spot. I moaned with pleasure.

He massaged me gently there with the tip of his finger while he continued licking my Hot Spot. The sensation of massaging my G-spot was nearly as strong as licking my clitoris, but he did them both together. The resonance of the two seemed to make the sensations even stronger than either by themselves.

This was way more than I could take quietly. I arched my back and moaned louder.

The forefinger of his other hand he drew across the skin between my Intro and my ass, massaging there as he went.

I moaned even louder and pounded my hands on the bed.

Then he inserted his second finger into my anus a little, went in and out some, and then back to massaging the area in between, then back to my anus again.

Tears filled my eyes. "Yes," moan after "Yes," moan escaped my lips, along with a lot of undecipherable noises as I pounded the bed.

Fingering my Pussy including my G-spot with one hand, fingering the area between my Intro and my ass, and then my ass with the other, all the while licking my Hot Spot... this is how a man should go down on a woman. That's all I'm saying.

When Juan finally rose up, and very slowly thrust his Cock completely into me with a decadently slow Full Sensation Thrust, I felt the warm waves of pleasure build as he filled me and when we finally exchanged our finishing hip rolls, I was overtaken by another Epicurean. It resonated through my entire body.

Just like Thomas and Will, making *Eros* love with Juan was indescribable. As the Epicurean started, I lost all track of time, and I only know it was a long time before he came and when he did, he pressed his Hilt firmly into my Hot Spot and rode his orgasm out right there.

Once again, I felt all the sensations of each short, hard orgasmic thrust, the warmth of my own orgasm spreading out to every part of me, the pulsing pumping of the shaft of his Cock, the glorious hotness of his cum exploding deep within me, accompanied by the unique sensations of a Squirts orgasm, his chest pressing on my breasts, his chest hair tickling my nipples, his Hilt pressing on my Hot Spot, they all merged into one family of sensations, another glorious Epicurean Experience.

After his orgasm, Juan stayed in me for a long time too, much longer than Will had. Probably this was because we had all evening. His lips caressed mine. His body pressed down on me, his chest massaged my breasts, his chest hair tickled my nipples, his warm thick Cock completely filled my Pussy, his Hilt pressed into my Hot Spot as he kept my Afterglow Orgasm going.

He just moved slowly, gently. He did not move his Cock in and out hardly at all; he let little movements of his body move him around, keeping me in a slow motion orgasm that took almost no energy for either of us to maintain. The intimacy overtook me and I had never felt more completely a woman in my life.

After a time, like with Will, it seemed like we'd been transported to some "other place," not exactly of this world, not exactly somewhere else. I had no idea which body parts were mine or his and didn't care. We stayed like this for three hours, and yes, I was orgasmic the whole time. Have you ever had a guy care about you enough to keep you going for three hours? Guys who revere the Divine Feminine can do this. One of Aphrodite's secrets is that if he never takes his Cock out of you, it will stay hard enough to do this for a very long time. The only question is how much he cares about you. That's all I'm saying.

When we were about an hour into the Afterglow, something special occurred, sort of like what had happened with Will only more so. We'd been in the wonderful "other place" for some time when I felt a sensation emanating from a distinctly feminine shape behind a barrier like some sort of door. It was the most intense sensation of love I had ever experienced. After a period of time which I could not measure, this feminine presence faded, but Juan and my connection and my orgasm continued. Three hours of unbridled Joy, punctuated by a visit from a feminine presence on the other side.

After we finally rolled apart, Juan looked over at me, "Did you feel her?"

"You felt her, too?" I exclaimed. It seemed astonishing that we both felt the same thing.

"Yes," he smiled.

"And you knew she was feminine?" I asked incredulously.

"Yes, this time," Juan nodded, "The feeling is always full of intense love, but not always feminine. About half the time it's masculine."

"Does it surprise you that we both felt the same thing?" I asked earnestly.

"Not anymore," Juan smiled broadly.

"Does this happen all the time?" I continued.

"Actually, no," Juan explained, "All of the priestesses and priests who've been here for a while have had numerous encounters like this, so they happen fairly often, but not all the time."

"Was it Aphrodite, the Divine Feminine?" I gushed.

"Or a feminine representative," he answered, "None of us really know. We have never been allowed to see beyond the barrier."

"It doesn't really make a difference," I mused, "Does it?"

"No," Juan agreed.

"This means Heaven is real," I observed. How else could this experience be interpreted?

"That's what I believe," Juan agreed simply.

After a bit, Juan got up, made us each another Hendricks Martini and got some cheese. We moved to the couch, tossed a light throw over ourselves and snuggled nude in front of the fire.

We had a lovely conversation lit by the flickering firelight. "Mary Ellyn," he began. "Do you know what happened here this evening?" he began.

"Yes," I answered, with no hesitation. "At least I think so. We made *Eros* love. The kind of love that begins in heaven and makes two people one, almost like our auras united or something."

He nodded slowly and smiled at me. "Yes," he agreed. "Our auras became one. How did you like it?"

I reached out and touched his cheek, softly, caressed his lips with mine, and then looked into his eyes, "It changes my understanding of making love, *Eros* or any other kind. I felt it with Thomas first, then more with Will, and now most of all with you. Adding the Afterglow at the end, actually seems to complete everything. But maybe fulfill is a better word."

Juan nodded, "Both work, don't they? By the way, one way we describe this sensation is being in our Love Bubble. It is because our joint aura is one large bubble."

"Good name," I agreed, "Anyway, once we were in our Bubble, it seemed like we were someplace else, I don't know exactly how to describe it, maybe somewhere between heaven and earth. I can't imagine we literally left here but... well... it almost seems like we did..."

"The Doorstep of Heaven," Juan interjected. "I know exactly what you mean, we all do. That's what we call it."

"The Doorstep of Heaven," I said softly, and laid my head on his chest, "Another good name."

We said very little for the next few minutes, just luxuriating in the closeness we had created. The oneness of our souls persisted long after our bodies separated.

Finally, he continued, "It's important for you to understand oral and anal sex, and how they fit into true *Eros* lovemaking. First, let me ask a question. Did you honestly like the anal sex?"

I drew in my breath as I thought about this. "Honestly, not really, Juan. It was OK, I guess. I didn't mind," I began, "but not nearly as nice as what we did later."

"When a woman has had an Epicurean and is being honest, that's a pretty normal response, Mary Ellyn." He smiled. "That's actually part of the point. Anal sex by itself is never as satisfying for a woman as the other advanced techniques we teach. There's nothing really wrong with it, but we don't do it much around here."

He got up from the couch and walked over to the freezer, got out the Hendricks bottle, made us more Martinis and got some more cheese.

"Calories aren't really an issue, as hard as we worked," he noted with a smile, "and we're not driving anywhere so if we get a little buzzed, no big deal."

Watching his spectacular naked body move around in the firelight was a treat. Guys may love Aphrodite for making women look terrific, but I love Jehovah for making men look like Juan.

"Oral sex," he continued after he returned and snuggled back under the throw, "with my Cock, like we did, is a way for you to give me pleasure"—and he flashed me a crooked little grin—"and you certainly did. But if we turn it into a blow job; where I cum in your mouth, you get very little out of that, and afterward, I have no way to give pleasure to you."

"So that is not making love?" I asked, "*Eros* or any other kind?"

He shook his head. "Anal sex, and blow jobs, no. Making *Eros* love always goes both ways."

That made sense. "Good," I said smiling.

"How did you like the way I went down on you?" he asked.

"Spectacular," came rolling out of my mouth unbidden. "I didn't know it could all be put together like that. I especially liked what you did with your one finger, moving between my Pussy and ass and massaging the area in between, mixed in with everything else you were doing. I've never been touched there before."

"It's called the taint," he said with a laugh.

"The taint?" I asked, my eyes wide open in surprise. "The place between my Pussy and my ass?"

"Yeah, that is what one of our first instructors called it. A red neck named Joe Bob from Georgia."

"Why did he call it that?"

"Taint exactly Pussy, and it taint exactly ass," Juan answered. We both got a good laugh from that one.

"Anyway... all put together... wow, is all I have to say. But it seems combining all of that would be hard for a guy," I said and kissed him. "I have two questions. First, did you enjoy going down on me like you did? Is it something men do just for us, or is it fun for you too?"

"Great question and you looking at it from my perspective says a lot about you. Being tuned completely to your partner is *Eros* love. To answer your question, absolutely." Juan laughed. "Every man I have ever known loves driving a girl crazy like that. It's more difficult, sure, but when we're connected like that, we feel it with you, so, it's actually thrilling for a guy to be able to do something like that for a woman."

"OK." I nodded. "I am starting to learn the importance of the emotional connection for guys. I'd always thought it was more for us, but obviously not. It never occurred to me that you would feel our orgasm like that."

Juan smiled and nodded, "The physical pleasure we feel in our Cock, but the emoticnal pleasure we feel all over just like you do."

"OK, next question. How is it that you found my G-spot so easily? I've only had three men get there before. Thomas, Brady and you. And Brady's new."

"There's a trick," he answered and gave me the finger. Literally, he did. He stuck out his middle finger and scrunched up the two next to it, flipped me a classic "bird" and laughed. "That's where this came from. You didn't know?"

"What?" I asked.

"Yeah," he answered. "If you make the finger like that and then insert it into a woman's Pussy, you are in the exact place of a woman's G-spot. The G-spot is on the forward wall. So, if I am laying next to you, make my finger like that and push it into you, my palm is up, and my middle finger is in perfect position to massage your G-

85

spot. Giving a girl 'the finger' started out as meaning a really good thing."

"You're kidding?" I laughed.

"No"—he insisted—"that's it. I make my finger like that, 'Give' it to you, by sticking it up into your Pussy until the fingers of either side bear on the outside of your Pussy, and then tickle your G-spot. Works for almost every girl."

"OKKKKK," I was still laughing. "One more question. How is it that you guys can maintain the level of sexual activity? I mean the number of times you can do it is phenomenal. Is there some trick or something?"

"No tricks. We take two special dietary supplements. The first makes a guy's Cock bigger, among other things and the second allows us to produce more semen. It means we can have more orgasms in a day than normal."

"I've always heard that size didn't matter?" I asked with a quizzical look on my face.

"That's only true for men who are moving too fast for a woman to feel the sensations build," Juan answered. "When a guy moves slower, the amount your Pussy and Intro are stretched does matter." He smiled. "So do more orgasms. Speaking of that..." Juan said as he took off the throw and kissed me softly.

"Let's go out to the beach." He smiled a knowing smile. "It's time for you to learn something wonderful."

"More wonderful than what I've already learned?" I asked.

"Maybe," he answered enigmatically, and he reached for my hand.

"Shall I throw a coverup on?"

"No need," was all he said. As we walked out through a path that led through the dunes, I noticed how feminine and free I felt walking naked with this man, here in this place. There were other people around, but they took no note of us, and we took none of them. The night was clear and bright and there was a brilliant full moon out that seemed near enough to reach out and touch.

Once we were out on the beach, Juan tuned to the right and we walked hand in hand on the wet sand with warm shallow surf washing past our feet as the waves came in. After we'd walked about a hundred feet, Juan stopped and turned to face me. "People all over the world have different ways to acknowledge and commune with their creator," he began, "and we have no criticism and nothing to take away from anyone's religious practices. We do have something to add. If you face the moon on a night like this, stand naked with your arms outstretched, palms forward and just drink in the heavens, something wonderful happens. You feel recharged, and women get something extra. You guys can commune with the Divine Feminine this way. Most women are aware of their intuition, but most don't really know what it is. Your intuition is actually Aphrodite speaking with you, helping you. When you commune with her like this, it strengthens your ability to hear her, makes her voice easier for you to understand. Afterwards, if you do this with a man and make *Eros* love afterwards it magnifies these feelings in you. We call this 'Aphrodite Intuition.'

"This doesn't work for men?" I shook my head in disbelief.

"No," Juan admitted a little sadly, "It's probably a right brain, left brain thing, but the intuition that you guys have and can develop is not something that men have at the same level. We get gut feelings about things, but it's not the same. Men have certain strengths and weaknesses, so do women. When it comes to this sort of intuition, it is one of your strengths, one of our weaknesses."

"OK." I nodded, "But most women don't really look at it as a 'strength' like that. Our intuition is a thing that comes whenever it comes, and most of us don't rely on it much."

"Mary Ellyn," Juan replied softly, "and with immense respect for women, it's because you don't develop it that you don't understand how to use it. This gift from Aphrodite doesn't develop quickly. Just like any other of our latent strengths, it has to be trained to become a true strength, but in time the priestesses here all say it is almost like being able to read minds. I've seen it with any number of priestesses and so will you. This is where it starts. Will you believe me, and try?"

His sincerity was simply over the top. I didn't really understand, but what do you say to a man who is so honest and sincere? "Yes, Juan," I leaned into him and kissed him gently, "I believe you, and will try."

We faced the moon, and stood there silently soaking up the essence of heaven. I felt the moonlight wash over me like any girl has, but this time I was consciously opening myself up to the heavens and it felt protective, wonderful in a new way. It would be some time before I began to notice my intuition getting more frequent, more reliable, but in time, I too came to believe that this was indeed the Divine Feminine speaking to us.

Juan and I turned, and hand in hand, he led me back toward the dunes where we found a bin of beach blankets. Juan got one and we went farther back, found a level place and spread it out. I folded myself into his embrace, and we began to make out. Kissing intermittingly and looking into each other's eyes and then up at the moon, savoring not just each other but the heavens as well. After a time we lay down, and Juan began a Venus Massage while he nibbled my closest nipple. This freed up my eyes to look up towards heaven, the moon and the stars.

Glorious!

This's all I'm saying. Laying on your back on the beach looking up at the heavens while a man is savoring you is a spiritual experience. Glorious is the only word for it. His finger moved down to my Intro, and he gathered moisture there and brought it up to my Hot Spot. He began gently massaging me there, and I "instinctively" knew that this was not the time or place for him to go down on me. Was this Aphrodite speaking to me? At the time I didn't know, but now, I think so, I really do.

We continued savoring each other for a delightfully long time, and then he rolled over between my legs, spread them wide and filled me with a wonderfully slow Full Sensation Thrust. We made sweet *Eros* love for an hour at least and then we shared his orgasm. He maintained the Afterglow for a long time and I will tell you that in my entire life I had never felt so close to the Cosmos, and when we found our way back to the bungalow, I slept the most restful sleep I could ever remember.

The next morning, Juan made *Eros* love with me in the shower. It was delicious, I wanted him so. You'd have thought that I'd had enough yesterday, but making *Eros* love a lot creates a craving and you want it over again… and then over again. As we were fixing breakfast, I wondered if men realized the dividends they would get if they put this much effort into making *Eros* love a lot of the time. We would wear them out.

Oh, how I love being a girl.

Not long afterward, we began our martial arts instruction. All priestesses of Aphrodite are well trained in Tae Kwon Do, the form of martial arts that Chuck Norris does. We believe all people should be in control of their lives, with no one able to take something from them that they don't wish to give. There were so many instances like this during our training that I could go on for days. Both Shannel and I had more fun with men in the two months of priestess training than we had in our entire lives before that point.

Suffice it to say that after two months there was nothing the same about either of us. Our facial expressions were different. They radiated sexy confidence. We didn't walk, we sauntered. We were comfortable in our bodies. We projected sexuality well. We knew how to help a man form an emotional connection with us, how to savor him and teach him to savor us.

We were excellent partners with any man we chose to be with, knowing exactly what they needed or wanted and why. We knew how to teach men to do things with us that we had never known could be done with women before. We'd learned how to wake a man at three a.m., make *Eros* love in the middle of the night, and give him what he wanted most… to feel wanted by his girl.

We spent time communing with the heavens in the moonlight and both of us had felt our Aphrodite Intuition developing. We knew when Aphrodite had something to say. Our confidence in our femininity overflowed. And overflowing feminine confidence makes every woman sexy in a way that no garment, pose, pair of tits, hourglass figure, or superficial feature can match. The finer points would take years, but we were now priestesses, and we were good at it. Really good at it. Chapter Three of our journey was complete.

We realize there are those who will disapprove of the manner we use, but that is their business. This is ours and we offer no apologies to anyone. Shannel and I had feasted on Aphrodite's fruit and knew it was the best fruit anyone could ever have. Oh, and I suppose I should mention that the Ben Wah Balls were an excellent idea. Oh yeah! Enough said!

As this chapter came to a close we were priestesses of Aphrodite, teachers of the Divine Feminine, and happy.

Chapter Five

Shannel and I had the time of our lives for several years, until one morning as I walked toward her bungalow, I felt my Aphrodite Intuition urging me to move faster. I was about to break out into a jog when I heard Claire call out to me from behind, so I stopped. Claire often had questions about the San Dan testing she was undergoing. I answered her questions, turned and began to jog towards Shannel's bungalow. My intuition let me know things were not good and to hurry, so I ran faster and as I approached her door, I received the shock of my life. A sensation well known from my martial arts training wafted across my senses.

Danger Close!

I quickly threw open her door and walked in. Shannel lay naked on the bed, her wrists and legs bound to the bedposts. She was in a spread-eagle position, and a creampie oozed from her Intro. I noticed some sort of red ball in her mouth attached by a strap around the back of her head and neck so she could not spit it out. It looked like some sort of BDSM thing, but I don't do that, so I don't really know. I do know there was no way she could have screamed.

It looked to me like Shannel had been bound to the bed, rendered silent, and raped. I am not a doctor by any means, but it was pretty clear my friend wasn't breathing. I immediately crossed the room and started CPR. It was to no avail. My dear friend was dead. There came the sensation again.

Danger Close!

Stronger this time, plus Aphrodite was screaming to be careful, things would come to a head quickly. The change in the room's aura was unmistakable.

Danger Close!

Bound like she was, there was no way for her to activate the alarm in the necklace we all wore. I had already activated mine. Security would be arriving shortly.

Danger Close!

Whoever did this was still nearby. I felt certain of it. I had to get a grip. I had to focus.

There was a towel twisted up laying beside her and it looked like it might have been used to strangle Shannel. Not my issue at the moment... *"FOCUS, Mary Ellyn, get it together and FOCUS!"* I told myself. There it was again.

Danger Close!

During the time, when I was being trained in the mastery of the techniques and philosophies of Sam Dan, my Sensei would blindfold me with a black blindfold, walk silently around me, and throw punches I couldn't see. You have to focus, first on yourself and the Zen concepts of non-violence, and then expand your focus. As you do so, if your focus is proper and your concentration correct, you can feel things that are contrary to the non-violence of your persona. As you gain experience you can feel the contrary aura's movements. This translates into being able to sense the location of danger without being able to see it. Being able to sense auras you can't see and tell whether that person intends to do harm is a significant part of being a Third Degree Black Belt. I am Sam Dan. I passed this test. It is not possible to surprise someone like me… if… we clear our mind and focus. The problem at the moment was the shock of seeing my lifelong friend dead, had interfered with everything.

Shannel hadn't quite yet completed her second degree, called Ni Dan. If her attacker had surprised her, it would explain how he had succeeded. FOCUS! *"Get it together, Mary Ellyn, and FOCUS!"* I said to myself again. There it was once more:

Danger Close!

There was a killer on the loose and if I didn't get it together and focus, I would be next. I put my grief aside, cleared my mind of all emotion, and focused. As I did, everything resolved. The Danger Close sensation was coming from the bathroom. Shannel's murderer was there, preparing to attack me, and he had a weapon of some kind. Beyond that I did not know. Higher levels than Sam Dan could have filled in more information, but I had all I needed to be prepared. I moved off of the bed and faced the bathroom door about ten feet away. This was the first time I could remember my martial arts training and my Aphrodite Intuition working together. I knew from Aphrodite that the door would open any second, but I also heard her telling me I would be able to handle this.

Suddenly, a naked man stepped out. I immediately noticed that he was in excellent physical shape and had a Kevlar knife in his right hand.

Good, I thought, *right handed, and that hand occupied with a knife*. No knife was ever going to be useful against a woman of my skill level. As he looked at me, his Cock became erect. Given the skin-tight nature of my outfit and the way it hugged my breasts, my ass, and my Pussy; I was sexy to any binary man with a pulse. *Good*, I thought again. Those emotions were only going to be a distraction for him.

"Well," he said with a leering smile, "I was hoping to have my way with two of you Heretics. Looks like I will get my wish." He gestured to me. "Dressed as you are, you're practically as naked as she is," he said, pointing toward Shannel. "It is an abomination to God himself for you to dress like this and it is time now for you to be punished. Do you want to do this the painless way and take your clothes off, or do you want to make me cut them off of you?"

"Neither," I answered calmly as he started to move toward me. It was time to do something he did not expect.

I took a step toward him.

One of the things about the Zen portion of martial arts training is the way we handle fear. We don't deny it, but we put it behind us. We never show it. This jacks with your adversaries' head. Here am I… a "girl," the weaker sex, unarmed; and here is he… a "macho man" in great physical shape, much stronger than any "girl," and he has a knife. In his world view, I'm supposed to crumble into a ball of paralyzed fear, and just submit. Instead, as he moved toward me, I moved toward him.

A very debilitating thing happens in the head of your assailant when they think you should be afraid, and clearly you are not. It raises questions, creates uncertainty. In his mind, this "girl" is supposed to be terrified, but she's not. Why? Good question. That question hinders him… a lot. He just doesn't know it, and that is a good thing. The look of increased concentration and confusion on his face as I took the step toward him meant I was having the desired effect.

"Your choice then," he said through gritted teeth as he got into position to make a lunge thrust with the knife. I noticed his motions, and they were not crisp. There was some hesitation there. This guy was certainly in good shape, but he did not move like someone with a lot of training. My single step forward would have had some effect on a well-trained man, but not this much.

He started his lunge thrust. This is the normal tactic for someone with a knife. Only a fool tries to slash you. A lunge thrust is a straight, belt-level thrust with the intent of burying the knife straight into your gut. Dealing with a lunge thrust is nothing complicated for a woman like me. I did the normal Level One response and… just… took a step back.

That's all. One step back.

This simple act, timed properly, throws your assailant's balance off and jacks with his confidence even more.

My timing was perfect.

He very nearly stumbled, and I smiled.

"Oh," he sneered, "you think that's funny, do you. You'll find out what's funny soon enough."

"I'm going to rape you," he sneered, "And then I am going to slowly choke the life out of you, and the last thing you will feel as you leave this world will be my dick in your cunt." This was his attempt to intimidate me.

"Good Luck with that," I said casually, as if he were of no more challenge than a small child. One of the best things that can happen in this situation is if your assailant tries to intimidate you, and can't.

The man regained his balance, but not all of his confidence, which was the point of a Level One response. He took another step forward to fill the gap I'd created and prepared to make another lunge thrust with the knife. Now was the time for a Level Two response.

Do you remember the movie Karate Kid? "Wax on and wax off" are actually blocks to deflect anything aimed higher than your belly button. The "sand the floor" moves portrayed in the movie are blocks for anything aimed lower. These blocks are some of the most basic and well-practiced martial arts moves in Tae Kwon Do.

He made his thrust straight at my belly, and I did a simple "sand the floor" with a "snap" at the point of contact, which was the back of his knife hand. It is the "snap" on contact that allows a martial artist, female or male, to break boards or bricks. The point of being able to break boards or bricks is not to break them. Who would care about that? Once we learn to break boards, we can break bones if we need to, and that is the point. The "snap" broke several bones in his hand and knocked the knife flying. It was easy. Almost absurd.

The confusion on his face was actually clearer than the pain from his broken hand. How had a girl disarmed him, and shattered his hand? Even more, he was supposed to be under God's protection. Clearly that was not the case.

The truth was this; the fight was over. The only question was how I would finish it off. I could kill him with one punch to the base of his nose, driving the nasal cartilage up into his brain. It was an easy move for me to do, but if I killed him our security people couldn't ask questions, so I opted for a different route.

Keep the murderous bastard alive.

I could crush his windpipe with a "knuckle chop" which is a crossing left to right uppercut with the knife edge of your knuckles to the windpipe, but that would require immediate medical attention to keep him alive. What if it didn't arrive in time?

Instead, I used a "knuckle knife punch." I formed my right hand, not into a fist, but where the intermediate knuckles are fully forward, with the tips of your fingers curled around to the top of the palm of your hand and the intermediate knuckles are sort of like a knife. This is the same configuration you would use for a "knuckle chop" to the throat, but it's a punch instead. This type of punch is called a "knuckle knife punch."

I took a long step forward with my left leg. The punch was with my right hand, timed with the forward step, so the punch incorporated the power of my legs... and... my arm. The punch was toward the upper portion of his gut, about six inches under his ribs on his left side and as the punch lands your fist twists counterclockwise, hard. The punch along with the twist, takes all of the breath out of your adversaries' body, racks him with indescribable pain, and if properly delivered, tears the abdominal musculature, ruptures his spleen, and ends the fight. It does not, however, require immediate medical assistance.

My knuckle punch was perfectly delivered. After delivering the blow, I took another step back. His face was contorted in pain, shock, and complete surprise. He was trying to breathe, stand upright and not doubled over, but not doing a good job. No one had ever hit him like that or caused him such pain. Further, it was beyond his comprehension that this could be done to him by a "girl."

Guys like this are always surprised by how powerful the female gender can be. This is a stupid mistake to make.

He was clearly incapable of further action, but he was still standing. I delivered a vicious side kick to the center of his chest, knocking him backward and flat on his back. A kick like that, properly delivered, will dislocate several of the ribs where they attach to the sternum and break one or two on each side. It is extremely painful.

My kick was properly delivered.

As my assailant rolled on the floor in excruciating pain, his movements brought him close to the knife. He picked it up in his left hand, but before he could do anything, I sprung across the room landing on the solar plexus of his abdomen with the knee of one leg and on the wrist of the knife hand delivering a "snap kick" with my other foot, shattering the other wrist. I reached out and yanked the knife out of his hand, jumped back to my feet, moved back and waited for security.

I watched him intently as he tried to grapple with the intensity of the pain. Normally, I hated it when something I had done hurt someone. I have no interest in hurting anyone, but I felt no sorrow or sympathy, keenly aware that my best friend was on her bed, dead by this man's hand. Why hadn't Aphrodite warned Shannel I wondered, and then I remembered. Shannel had a heart of gold. She would have responded to the warning by trying to help her student. Tears moistened my eyes as I remembered the kind, precious soul who had been ripped from us.

I had known Shannel since we had been cheerleaders together all through high school. We were roommates all through college. We were taught to be priestesses here at Fantasy Bay together. She was my best friend, and now she was gone... forever. The combination of anger and sadness tempted me to go over and just break the man's neck. I certainly knew how, but knowledge of how to do something does not mean you should. We needed whatever information this man had, so I stood where I was and waited for Security to arrive.

I could see him trying to use his anger at what I had done to him to overcome his pain, gather his strength, and attack me again. I hoped he would. It would give me the justification to hurt him again, and maybe succumb to the temptation to kill him. I hated feeling this way, but when your best friend is dead it's hard to feel differently about her murderer.

Just then two armed security agents burst through the door, weapons drawn. They were trained to take our alarms seriously. Alarms almost never happen, because there is rarely a reason for them too, but when they do, these guys are ready. After looking at Shannel, one looked at me and asked, "Are you OK, Miss Mary Ellyn?" I nodded. He meant physically, not emotionally. "Is there anyone else around?"

"No," I answered evenly. The other guard looked at the guy flopping about on his back. His breathing was labored, and he was in great pain. "Thanks for keeping him alive for us."

I was about to reply when the assailant on the ground rolled his lower lip over his lower teeth and bit down. His eyes rolled into the back of his head; and he died.

"Cyanide," one of the security guards said as he felt for a pulse in the man's jugular vein, "or something like it."

The other one looked at Shannel, walked over and felt her pulse, bowed his head, sighed and softly said, "Oh, no."

The first guard nodded and their eyes met. "Those assholes must have gotten one through." Even in my emotional state, I wondered who "those assholes" were.

Chapter Six

Once the police had left, I insisted on knowing who "those assholes" were. The people who had "gotten one through." Our security people made no mention of them to the police. I was told there was a group of religious zealots who had threatened us about a year ago, but other than their name, little was known about them. They called themselves the "Foundation for Righteousness." They had demanded that we cease teaching that God had both a masculine and a feminine nature; cease teaching men how to please women, and instead teach men how to bring women into submission. According to them, the function of a woman was to please a man, regardless of whether he pleased her or not. We paid no attention to their demands. Nothing had come of it until now.

After the police and security had debriefed me, I'd gone back to my bungalow. As I sat on my couch teary eyed, wandering through the memories of my friend Shannel, I realized in about ten minutes, Brian, my Mon Chéri, would be back. At Fantasy Bay, priestesses like me are dedicated to teaching men to be really good lovers. We are paired with a man for one week, called our Mon Chéri. Your Mon Chéri stays in your bungalow and takes daily lovemaking classes with you every morning. The first thirty minutes were normally a demonstration of a particular lovemaking skill, then we go back to our bungalow and spend an hour practicing whatever was being taught that particular day.

Afterward, we separate for the remainder of the day and meet back in the bungalow at nine in the evening. We spend the night together, and usually practice the morning lesson again. The opportunity to practice with a live instructor who knows exactly what she's doing is one of the keys to our success.

After the week of instruction, the guests, half men, being trained by priestesses, and half women, being trained by priests, go to a different set of bungalows, for a second week and use the *Eros* lovemaking techniques they have learned with each other as they enjoy the resorts amenities.

In spite of what had happened to Shannel, I was not going to stand Brian up. Teaching men how to emotionally connect with women, and all of the things they could really do with us was a part of my identity. Shannel's murderer was not going to take this away.

As I sat on my own bed, I knew I had to tell this story. Shannel was a good girl. So was I. So were all of us here, though there were people who might disagree. Did that justify killing us? I knew then this story had to be told. It was time for who we are and what we believe to come out into the light. I made my resolution as Brian walked into my bungalow.

A short time later, we walked into the classroom hand in hand. Yesterday was Brian and my first day together. We were Introduced at noon, had lunch in a Tiki Bar, went back to my bungalow and got him settled in. We'd had sex four times already. First beside the pool at my Bungalow, then, after dinner out on the beach, and later as we went to bed, then in the middle of the night, I rolled him over, mounted him Girl-On-Top and screwed his brains out.

Sunday was a nice day for us both, but today was our first class together. Sunday is the only day when we have what we consider "sex" with our Mon Chéri. At that point, the guests don't really understand the difference between "having sex" and "making *Eros* love." Developing this understanding would start today. There would be a discussion, then a demonstration. Afterward, each couple would go back to her bungalow, and practice what had been demonstrated.

Today was basic foreplay, accompanied by "Full Sensation Thrusts." Brian and I settled into a pair of chairs in the demo theater, and a few minutes later, Will and Helena walked onto the stage. These were the instructors who would teach and demonstrate the lesson. There were a variety of cameras set up along with a number of large screens so everyone could see from every angle.

The first part of the lesson was basic foreplay, essentially nothing new other than the importance of being slow and making sure the guys understood the value of letting the sensations they created build to their peak "for her" before moving on to something else. Exactly how a man would know "for her" would be a recurring theme. "So, as important as this is," Will said clearly, "now we move on to the next part of today's lesson. 'Slow' is not just about hands. It's about a man's Cock as well. We call it Full Sensation Thrusting. The position is Missionary, but the concept can be applied in a lot of ways. The point of what we will show you is this... a slow uninterrupted stroke with full penetration and a firm finish is the most wonderful thrust of a man's Cock a woman can experience. All of you guys have seen porno films. What you see there is... not... how good lovers make love. All you ever see in those videos is screwing. What Helena and I will demonstrate today is making *Eros* love... it is infinitely better, enough said."

He continued by explaining that a man's Hilt was the part of his anatomy directly above his Cock, and that it was ideally positioned to stimulate a woman's Hot Spot... if... the thrust was a full penetration and finished with a hip roll up. He continued by explaining that one of the characteristics of all good lovers was the ability to use their Hilt to stimulate a girl's Hot Spot.

"There are two reasons for this," he concluded. "First is the excellence of the clitoral stimulation when you do this for a woman, but second, a woman's Cervix is usually three to five inches in. The Pussy's walls begin to stretch when a man's Cock comes into contact with her Cervix. As he continues to penetrate her it stretches out her Pussy. Done fast this can hurt some women, but done slow, it is stimulating. Many women have had some bad experiences with deep penetration, and cervical contact. This is because the man involved did not know what he was doing. Now this is a big key. If you do foreplay well, penetrate her slowly, connect with her Cervix gently, and stretch her out very slowly, you will not hurt her, and she will love it. Repeated deep penetration produces a cervical orgasm that will be simultaneous with her clitoral, Intro, and G-spot orgasms. The four happening together is called an Epicurean Experience which is fantastic for a woman, but there is a catch. If your thrust is too fast or too hard it can hurt your partner, and that is not what we want to do. A slow thrust will never hurt her and only accentuates her pleasure."

"Immensely!" Helena said as she took over. "The optimum time for a man's first stroke into a woman's Pussy is about five or six seconds," she began. "A man's thrust has four distinct sensations for a woman. The first happens when the head of his Cock opens her Intro as he enters." She looked around the hall and smiled. "The name of the entrance to a Woman's Pussy is Introitus, but we call it her Intro. You can think of it as the spot where a man Introduces a woman to his Cock." That brought a few chuckles.

Helena continued, "The second is when the Head passes her G-spot, the third and fourth are the ones Will just described. It takes a little time for each of the first two sensations to build. If a man does the stroke slowly, each sensation builds to its highest level, and then persists for a short time. It's still at its peak when he engages her Cervix with the head of his Cock, and her Hot Spot with his Hilt. The combination of these four sensations comes together to make what is much more than a simple orgasm. We call it an Epicurean Experience. There are four keys. A man's stroke has to be slow, her legs have to be spread wide, he has to ride in low, it has to be as deep as possible, and it has to be one continuous uninterrupted stroke, so the first two sensations from the Intro and G-spot do not dissipate before the next two kick in."

"OK," Will said jumping back in. "Here's the last thing for today, and that's the way you finish. When you feel your orgasm about to begin, you make one final thrust and hold pressure with your Hilt against her Hot Spot. You let your orgasm come to her. What happens when you do this is; she feels every one of your short orgasmic thrusts in both her Hot Spot and her Cervix, she feels the heat as your cum explodes into her, and she is connected to your orgasm. Nothing you can do for a woman while making *Eros* love is better for her than this. There are many things that are just as good. We'll get to these as the week goes on, but letting her experience your orgasm with you is one of the keys to being a great lover."

During the demo we watched them engage in foreplay, and then when they were ready, Will placed his Cock into the Intro of Helena's Pussy, letting it nestle there for a few seconds, then pressing firmly, yet slowly until he was all the way in, and his Hilt came into firm contact with her Venus Mons and pressed into her Hot Spot. He stayed pressed there for a couple of seconds, then withdrew about halfway and thrust slowly all of the way back into her until he stimulated her Hot Spot. He did this three times, then pulled all the way out, and slowly repeated the process. One full deep stroke, followed by three shorter strokes, but not pulled out very far and finished just as deep.

As was normal in these demos, Brian's full attention was on the camera angles that showed Will's Cock barely inserted into Helena's Labia, and then ending fully thrust into her Pussy. I get this. Brian was admiring Helena's Pussy. There is nothing to be gained by women bitching about boys being boys. Brian would come around in time. They always did, but sometimes it was a process. At least I hoped he would. My Aphrodite Intuition was telling me to be careful. I was always more interested in the expression on Helena's face, and how it grew more rapturous with each Full Sensation Thrust. Her face told the real story. This was clearly a woman enraptured by what was happening. When his orgasm happened, Will held right there, and you could see what was happening to Helen play across her face.

Making *Eros* love this way is not about making a guy "feel" great directly. The thing is this; as long as they have established an emotional connection to begin with, the joy the woman experiences draws him into her. Not in a physical sense but an emotional one. Her joy sucks him in and her he feels her pleasure. He might even think the sensations he's feeling are coming from her Pussy, but they're not. Each partner is doing what they are doing for the other. They are making *Eros* love. The sensations he's feeling are coming from her soul and before long they create their own Love Bubble.

One thing I admired was how Fantasy Bay got these men into the emotional side of making *Eros* love on Day One. From that point forward we were no longer having sex together but making *Eros* love together.

Brian and I went back to my bungalow after the demo and sat on the couch. We always talk for a while first. Then we kissed for a few minutes and started the basic foreplay.

After a few minutes, Brian and I stood up, and he undressed me. This was easy. He pulled the camisole part of my negligée over my head, untied my bra and slipped it off, and then untied my panties. It was smooth and effortless.

I was standing nude before him... long blond hair, shoulders back, firm D's pointing straight at him, twenty-five inch waist, thirty-seven inch hips, long legs spread apart, bald Pussy, looking like a picture from a men's magazine.

A vision like this was normally enough to inspire any guy, but there was something a little off with Brian. I had no idea what it could be for sure. He had seemed unusually shy yesterday, and now again today so I decided to play it that way. It could also be guilt, but we treat them both the same. There is nothing wrong with a man being shy or feeling guilty. Priestesses just have to help get them past it, that's all. I reached behind him, untied and removed his G-string. There was nothing wrong with his Cock. He was as hard as a rock. He reached across me and fondled my nipple opposite the side he was lying on. He did it slowly, nicely.

After a short time, he stopped kissing me and began suckling my other nipple. The one closest to him. He moved his hand down to the top of my Venus Mons and stroked it while he suckled my breast. Then ran his finger down slowly to my Intro, gathered moisture and then up to my Hot Spot in pretty much classic form, just like the demo. After a bit, he rose, moved my legs apart, kneeled between them and began by kissing my Pussy, then licking my Hot Spot.

Once he had my orgasm going nicely, he placed his Cock at my Intro and got ready to thrust into me. Brian did not get his Cock all the way in me in one thrust the first try. He had to try three times, but he eventually got it. The third time he was able to do it, slowly pull all the way out, pause, then thrust slowly back in, taking almost six seconds and finishing with a nice strong drive of his Hilt into my Hot Spot and pausing there for a couple seconds. Next came several short strokes, followed by a glorious full one, over and over again.

He had his orgasm after about five minutes, and continued for about five more minutes and then, inexplicably, he was done. Once Brian got it right, I felt him deeply, enjoyed him thoroughly, and expressed my joy completely. Loud moans and pounding the bed with her arms is a dead giveaway a girl is really into it. He should have been enraptured in my joy. The emotional connection we were supposed to have should have made it hard for him to quit after ten minutes. The truth is that most guys never really want to quit unless they feel like that have to. So, what if he's had his orgasm, I mean, he's getting to slip his Cock into you over and over again. What, exactly, is not to like about this? Brian quit when he didn't have to. Perhaps the problem was he wasn't feeling the connection during foreplay. That was something I could work on with him. The only other explanation was he just didn't care about me.

After our morning practice session, each priestess and her Mon Chéri separate until about nine in the evening and go off to do whatever they want.

One of the resort's activities is scuba diving, and I love it. I love the sight of colorful fish swimming through the reefs and sea grasses, the tiny clown fish snuggling with the anemones, being semi-weightless in the warm clear water, and no sounds other than your own breathing.

After I left Brian, I tied on a red string bikini, and sauntered over to the dive center. As I approached, a dark-haired, grey-eyed guy came up to me. He was wearing a Black G-string and his muscles rippled as he moved. Very Nice!

"Hi, my name's Rob," he began.

"Mine's Mary Ellyn," I answered taking his hand and giving him a kiss.

We made small talk for a couple of minutes.

"Look," he said with some obvious nervousness after a minute, "You're a priestess, and I don't want to be a bother, but I haven't been out to the reef yet. If it's not too much trouble, could we go diving together and would you show me around out there? We don't have to do anything, just please, show me around."

I smiled pleasantly, "Rob, this is what we're here for. It's not a bother at all, and I'd love to show you around," I replied and touched his cheek, "And I'd love to make *Eros* love with you too. Are you dive certified?"

He nodded.

"This'll take a nice long time," I noted with another smile, "Shall we have lunch before we go?"

He agreed with another nod. This Tiki specialized in pizza, so we shared one and a pitcher of Yuengling beer. This is a Pennsylvania based brewery that is still owned by the Yuengling family, and the two family members running the company are women. At Fantasy Bay we like that, so we bring their beer all the way down here to Panama.

Once we finished our pizza and drained the last drop of beer, we checked out our scuba gear and boarded the dive boat. As we settled into our seats for the ride, Rob noticed an oblong clear Lexan bubble with a tube and regulator coming out of both ends. "What's that?" he asked.

"It's called a Fantasy Bay Air Bell," I answered. "It's a special dive chamber we can both get under together." I pointed to the silver tank and regulator. "That is the air supply and depth controller. Those electric propellers on each end move us around and those two sets of pads each rest on our shoulders. The straps over there go under our arms, so we don't slip out. The hose reels on the sides allow us to swim away and look around independently, if we want."

"Really?" he asked, clearly enthralled. He looked at me. "Why would we want to do that?'

"You'll see," I said with a suggestive smile. I looked over at the boat operator. "Is anyone at spot nine?"

"No, ma'am," he answered.

"Can you give is a tour and end up there?" I inquired.

"Of course," he replied with a knowing smile and headed the boat out in that direction.

After the tour, the boat operator dropped and secured the anchor by a buoy with a nine on it, then disappeared into the forward cabin. This wasn't his first rodeo. I slipped into Rob's arms and kissed him lightly, untied my top and removed it. I rubbed my nipples against his chest hairs for a minute or so, then untied my bottom, removing it too. I placed his hands on my ass, reached around behind him and untied his G-string. Just like that his hard naked Cock was riding against my soft naked Labia, his Hilt massaging my Venus Mons as I massaged his ass.

A naked embrace like this is a very nice way to make out with a man. It's delightful in a forest, especially when you can find something to lean against, but you can't go diving this way.

"Now do you see why we might want to be under the Air Bell together?" I asked as innocently as a naked girl in the arms of a naked man possibly can.

He nodded wordlessly.

"Shall we go?" I asked with a smile.

He nodded, still incapable of speech as he watched me move around naked and put on my flippers. I thought about how much I love being a woman and prick teasing a man as I folded the control arm down and we picked up the Air Bell and set it into the into water.

"See," I said pointing to the bottom skirt of the Air Bell as it floated next to our boat, "it rides down about eight inches. It will automatically keep the water level inside the Bell at that level."

I dove in and ducked under the Air Bell; Rob quickly followed. Once we were under, Rob looked at me with surprise. "We can talk!" he exclaimed.

I chuckled. "We can do a lot more than that." I leaned into him and tickled his tongue with mine. I operated the controller and we descended until we were about ten feet above the reef.

We found ourselves in the middle of an oceanic wonderland. Colorful fish were swimming through the reef coral, and vibrant anemones. There were many varieties of sea grasses, an entire saltwater biosphere, and the scene was beautiful, but Rob was not looking at the fish. He was swimming in clear warm water with a girl who was completely naked. The poor boy was trying to look at me. The problem was we were to close for him to get a good look. And I must admit, I am well enough evolved as a woman, to love being looked at, especially naked. One of the joys that Aphrodite gives girls is the one of putting on a show for guys, and I love doing it. The problem is when you are right next to a guy you can't put on a show, but I knew what to do about this.

There was a pouch on the control arm that had a special mixture of food that was good for eels. We liked to feed the eels so they wouldn't eat so many of the reef fish, and most of the priestesses knew where they lived. I unhooked the face mask on my side. "I'll be right back," I announced, "I have to feed the eel." And put the mask on.

"Feed the eel?" Rob asked.

The full face cover of the mask meant he couldn't hear me. "Watch," I mouthed, got the eel food, and I swam toward a cluster of rocks where I knew an eel lived. Now Rob was getting a really good look at a completely naked girl swimming in an oceanic wonderland, and that was the point.

I deposited the food where I knew the eel could detect it, backed off and watched. I loved to watch the eel come out and grab the food. After he ate it, he'd look at me for a few seconds, working his mouth like eels do, but I always imagined he was thanking me. During all of this, Rob was getting one of the best naked girl shows on the planet. I was completely naked, facing in his direction, keeping my shoulders back and slowly kicking with my legs about two feet apart and the setting was the resplendent glory of the reef biosphere. No burlesque troupe in history has ever put on a show like that.

After a few minutes, I swam back over to the Air Bell, stowed the mask and ducked back under, put his Cock back between my legs, put his hands back on my ass, took ahold of his ass and drew his Cock along my Labia until his Hilt came into contact with my Venus Mons. "There," I said tickling his tongue with mine, "isn't this nice?"

"I'll say," he replied, kissing me back.

This is the gentlest form of foreplay I know. Floating naked; weightless in an envelope of clear, warm, tropical water, surrounded by the kaleidoscope of colors of an ocean reef, kissing sensuously, my nipples being caressed by his chest hair; my ass being massaged by his hands; his ass being massaged by mine… his hard Cock moving slowly back and forth along my groove, his Hilt occasionally massaging my Venus Mons.

Glorious. A scene of beauty such as this could only have a divine artist, and the sensations of this foreplay for a girl could only have been designed by a Goddess. This is what is meant by divine.

This was our second day, but Rob already understood the idea of being slow and deliberate. That subject was part of the lesson this morning, but he already got it. He slowly pushed away, so his Cock would massage my groove in one direction then he pulled me back slowly rubbing me the other way, then finished by pulling me to him harder, driving his Hilt into my Hot Spot. A man doing this can actually get a woman's orgasm going very nicely without touching her Pussy with his hands or tongue at all. After a few moments, my orgasm was in full swing.

He moved his hips a little farther away, took a firmer grip on my ass and his Cock found my Intro. He kissed me softly as he paused. He started to draw me to him slowly, his Cock opened me, and thick warmness pushed in. The head of his Cock moved slowly past my G-spot, and those sensations joined together as he filled me deeper and deeper until he connected with my Cervix, then a bit more and a little bit more as he drew me closer and closer, stretching my Pussy to fit his Cock and then he filled me completely with a finial finishing thrust of his Hilt into my Hot Spot. A perfect thrust. Just like he had been taught that morning. Except weightless under a Fantasy Bay Air Bell. Slowly opening me, slipping in… allowing the sensations to peak… slip in farther to my G-spot… connect with my Cervix… slip all the way in… pause against my Hot Spot… slowly slipping all the way out, allowing me to close… pause then repeating… slowly… decadently… the only sound that of your breathing, the only sensations, the warm cocoon of tropical water, the vibrant colors, his lips on yours, his chest hair tickling your nipples, and the sensations his Cock creates in your Pussy. In a matter of a few moments, I had a full blown Epicurean going on.

Such an Experience in an environment like this is a form of heaven for which the basic concept of language fails. Finite words just never seem to communicate the true wonder you feel when you come into communion with the infinite. This is the reason we believe making *Eros* love is Godly, and a form of worship. It brings us into communion with the infinite.

After a little while I could feel his orgasm building. I drew him firmly into me, held his ass with my hands, pressed his Hilt into my Hot Spot and held him there as his hard short orgasmic thrusts took over our world.

Afterward, he kept my orgasm going. We had an hour's worth of air; we used it all.

It is in these moments, that I love being a woman the most.

After we had climbed back into the boat, and I had tied my bikini back on, I kissed Rob and looked into his eyes. "Now you know what it's like to go reef diving with a priestess."

"You've changed my life," Rob replied in a tone of awe and wonder.

This was not an uncommon response on these afternoon interludes when a priestess introduced a guy to something he'd never even imagined, let alone actually get to do with a real girl. "No," I answered with soft gentle tone and a knowing smile. "Aphrodite did."

Chapter Seven

One of the many things I love about being a priestess of Aphrodite is teaching a man the fine art of cunnilingus, otherwise vernacularly known as eating Pussy. Ever since my first evening here with Juan, I have loved having a guy eat my Pussy like he did that first night. Since I love it so, it's easy to imagine why I like to teach this to men, and this was the subject of the day's lesson.

After the demo, Brian and I went back to my Bungalow. As we settled onto the love seat at the foot of my bed, I could sense a deep unease, a buried darkness. It was well covered, but it was there. There are a lot of things which are difficult to hide from people who have developed Aphrodite Intuition.

OK, I thought to myself, *I don't know enough to know what this means, all I can do is my best.* For the moment, I was going to assume this was a bad case of shyness, but I was well aware it could be something darker. Aphrodite was telling me to be careful, but people like me don't assume the worst without evidence, Aphrodite's Intuition notwithstanding. I had no evidence of anything other than Brian being extremely shy, so there was no action to take other than to keep trying. I would be careful though. Women who learn to listen to Aphrodite Intuition have an advantage that is not to be given away lightly. We talked about the class a little bit. While the goal is to teach that spending time talking on the love seat is a time for communication, we only have a week so we don't try and go much deeper than the day's lesson.

I turned toward him and started to lean in. He met me halfway like I had shown him, and I kissed him. He kissed me back and we made out for a few minutes. We got up, went back to the bedroom, and I went over and laid down on the bed. He lay down beside me, and we started kissing again. He began stroking my breast through the negligee, then he took it off. He traced his finger slowly around the bra several times then untied it, first behind my neck and then in the back. He took it off and started to suckle my nipple closest to him as he traced his finger around my panties. He did this several times, then untied and removed them. His G-string soon followed.

He rose, spread my legs and laid down between them. He kissed me directly over my Intro, then slowly licked me up along my Labia, his tongue touching the bottom and passing over my Hot Spot, all the way up to the top. He did this several times, then started concentrating on my Hot Spot. He took the middle finger of his right hand and found my G-spot, exactly as he had been taught. With his other hand, he stroked firmly downwards slowly over my taint ending at my ass, and then back up to my Pussy, then back to my ass.

The interesting thing I realized in hindsight, was he never inserted his finger into my ass. He did a good enough job of massaging my G-spot and taint. Except for my ass, he was doing exactly like the demo, but he left something out. Was this intentional? If so, why? I didn't know but Aphrodite did and I would soon enough.

When you have a guy eating your Pussy like this, your orgasm is going to start up quickly. Once this happens, there are two problems for men. First, a woman can't lie still. The pleasure is so intense you move your hips whether you want to or not, and the guy's head is where it belongs at a time like this... between your legs. Can he match your movements and keep his action going?

The second is this, after about five minutes, ten at the most, you are going to begin to beg. You might or might not say the words, but your actions, the moans you make, the cry in your voice will make your desire clear.

You are saying, "Take me NOW!" There are many times when a good lover will pay attention to his partner, for her pleasure, but this is not one of them. Good lovers stick with eating their lover's Pussy, moving with her as she moves, and ignoring her pleas. Really good lovers don't stop until she begs him a number of times. Great lovers are going to keep this up for at least thirty minutes, no matter what the woman says or does.

But the man has to be able to say "no" to do this. It's about control, because a woman is going to beg with both her movements and her voice. No woman can simply lay still and quiet in the middle of a man eating her like this. Not even a priestess. To take a woman as far as this can take her, to let these sensations build to their natural crescendo requires time. To take a woman as high as she can fly, a man has to have the control to say no. As it turned out, Brian was unable to keep it going very long. Once I started to move, and especially moan, he rose up, slowly filled me, and we had a nice few minutes, but not nearly what could have been. Still, this was the morning class, and I knew we could try again tonight. Even so, it was frustrating. Not so much that he didn't keep going long enough, but that the look in his eyes was unsettling, almost vacant like he was somewhere else, though I could not yet explain why.

I had never had that reaction from a guy before. It was like something was not allowing him to enjoy this fully. Men love eating Pussy, and there is something magical about withdrawing their Cock until the head is resting barely inserted into a girl's Intro, then slowly driving it all the way in, and feeling the joy of the girl in his arms. The sensation of a girl laying back spreading her legs and giving a man every bit of Pussy she's got is intoxicating for men, and they don't quit until they are worn out to exhaustion.

Every guy I had ever been with at Fantasy Bay loved this. Every one of them. Without exception. But Brian just did not seem into it. I was beginning to wonder if he actually liked girls. Something just did not add up, but I didn't know what. Normally, my Aphrodite Intuition was pretty clear, but with Brian it was a jumble of mixed messages, with a measure of danger thrown in.

As we went our separate ways, I decided to go to the pool nearest my Bungalow. I went up to the waitress and ordered shrimp risotto and pointed to the table I was headed to. If you go around the pool toward the deep end, you are indicating that you would like a guy to approach you before you get into the water. If you go around the other way, toward the shallow end, you are indicating that you want to get into the water first. On their first day, after their mandatory intake physical and STD check, the guys are briefed on a number of things. This is one of them.

I sauntered around the pool toward the shallow end, tossed my hat and sunglasses on a lounge, removed my coverup, replaced my hat and sunglasses and sauntered naked over to the stairs leading into the pool's shallow end. I entered the pool and walked slowly through the water to a pair of slightly submerged lounge chairs. They were separated by a table that was out of the water and which supported an umbrella that shaded both lounges. I sat down and reclined on one.

A guy walked up to me and smiled. He was a blond, blue-eyed version of Rob Lowe, about six foot two, maybe two hundred pounds, with a lithe six pack, nicely formed pecks. His arm and shoulder muscles rippled seductively.

"Hi," he said with a dazzling smile. "My name's Tom. May I sit down?"

"Mary Ellyn," I said taking his hand. "Please do," I answered.

He sat down and looked over at me. "Could I get you a drink?" he inquired pleasantly.

"I'd love one," I answered. "How about a Hendricks Martini, dry, up, with three cocktail onions."

"Wow," he said impressed. "My kind of drink. Does that mean you're my kind of girl?"

"Possibly," I answered coquettishly. "I have shrimp risotto ordered. There will be enough for two."

"Sounds great. I'll be back in a minute with our drinks," he said rising and moving quickly through the water toward the stairs.

A few moments later I walked out, took off my coverup and met him as he returned. He handed me my Martini doing his best not to look like a deer caught in the headlights.

I took a small sip. "Perfect."

"They are, aren't they," he agreed. "I already tried mine. I wasn't going to bring yours over till I was sure they had it right."

"Thanks," I replied appreciating his consideration. If a woman is going to order a drink like that, it means she knows exactly what she wants, and classy men are going to make sure she gets what she wants.

We walked back to the table, I sat cowgirl in his lap, my Pussy about six inches from his erect Cock, ran my fingers through the hair at his temple and gave him a nice tongue tickle.

Just then, the waiter arrived with the risotto.

We began feeding each other shrimp and risotto. I love the way men make me feel when I prick tease them like this.

I love the looks, the way their desire cascades across their faces, the wonderful hardness of their Cocks, everything. I love it. If I was not going to finish what I started, it would make me the meanest bitch on the planet, but I do finish it, finish it well, always, and maybe that makes me one of the nicest girls on the planet.

Guys positively love for us to run Girlie Girl on them, drive them nuts and then deliver on the promise. Keep in mind, girls, if you want all he's got, you should give him all you've got. If he wants you to prick tease him shamelessly, and then lay back and let him drive you crazy… well… what's wrong with that? After the risotto was gone, we made small talk for a few minutes. "Would you like to go back to one of the pavilions?" Tom asked finally as we finished our drinks.

"Yes, I was really hoping you would ask." I answered simply, standing up and offering him my hand.

We walked back, selected a pavilion, and drew the drapes closed. I slid into his ready embrace, wrapped a leg around him, and he kissed me. We made out like this for a bit, I removed his G-string, and we made out some more, this time with his hard Cock riding against my soft Labia.

"May I ask you a favor?" he inquired nicely.

"Just about anything," I answered. What else was a totally naked girl in a completely naked man's embrace going to say?

"Can we do Girl-On-Top?"

"Sure. Why?"

"I want to look at you some more, a lot more actually," he answered honestly with a smile and a shrug. "Around the pool was not enough."

I smiled back at him. "OK, we can do that, and thanks for the compliment, but we haven't taught you about Girl-On-Top yet."

"What's to teach?" he asked.

"Well, for one thing, we don't start in that position," I replied, "because it doesn't work well for foreplay. Yes, I can straddle you, ride back and forth along your Cock and get my Pussy wet, but that isn't the primary goal of foreplay."

He nodded, remembering the lesson. "I see," he agreed. I nodded. "And it's hard to finish well like that,

124

both for men and women, so normally, we don't end that way."

"But it's great in the middle?" he asked.

"Absolutely," I replied coquettishly.

"What would you like me to do when we get to the middle?" he wanted to know.

"Earn it before we get to the middle, then lay back and enjoy the show," I answered, and kissed him again.

Oh, how I love being a woman and the things I can do for a man.

Tom eased me down, laid me on my back and began toying with my nipples as he kissed me softly. He took his time, allowing the joy to build. He began suckling and nibbling my nipple and moved the hand that had been massaging my other nipple down to my Venus Mons. This is an excellent place to massage a woman if you want to let her know you're not in a hurry, so Tom's instincts were perfect. But we hadn't taught the men how to properly massage a woman there yet. One of the nice things about being a priestess is that you can accelerate the lesson if you want.

"Here," I said gently, "do it like this." I showed him my three middle fingers together. I took his hand and placed it pointed down, about three inches up from my Venus Mons, pushed it so it applied gentle pressure, and then moved it down all the way to where my Pussy turned and then about a half inch past with his middle finger following my Labia. Then back. He caught on immediately.

I drew in my breath. "Oh, that's nice, Tom." I exhaled. The sensations of having your nipple suckled while your Venus Mons is stroked this way, over and over, is luxurious.

After about ten minutes, his hand inched farther and farther down. The tantalizing buildup of anticipation is delicious. You know he is about to start massaging your Hot Spot and each stroke of his hand takes him a little closer, but yet you have to wait. When he finally reached my Hot Spot he realized it wasn't quite wet enough, so he went on past it to my Intro, gathered my natural lubricant, brought it up and took me to the next level.

After a bit, he rose up, placed his hands on my knees and spread my legs wide, went down on me, and began eating my Pussy, his tongue licking slowly up from my Intro across my Hot Spot, and then all the way to the top of my Labia a couple of times then concentrating on my Hot Spot, his finger on one hand in my Pussy massaging my G-spot, the finger of his other hand massaging my taint and my ass perfectly. I started to move and moan, and then moan louder.

Tom was perfect. He ate my Pussy for about thirty minutes. It was exquisite. It takes a lot of internal strength as well as commitment to the woman for a man to have this kind of control. He'd earned everything I could do.

Eventually, he rose up. I sat up, rolled him over onto his back, placed one of my knees outside of his knee, seductively moved my other knee to the outside of his other knee and straddled his legs like a cowgirl. I let him take it all in for a minute, then bent over and took the tip of his Cock into my mouth. I sucked a little and he moaned. I slowly licked his Cock all the way down the body to his balls, kissed them, tickled his scrotum with my tongue, licked back up to the head of his Cock, and took as much of him into my mouth as I could. I tightened my lips and went up and down his Cock several times. As I took it out, I sucked the head again until he moaned. I sat up and smiled at Tom, moved up a bit so my Groove trapped his Cock and rode back and forth a bit, using his Cock to play with my Hot Spot. Finally, I took his Cock in my right hand, put the tip of its' head into my Intro and paused.

This is an exceptionally sexy pose for guys. Your shoulders are back, your breasts thrust out, your legs spread wide, your Pussy in full view, with his Cock nestled in prime position… this is a vision of a girl no guy will ever forget.

It is moments like this one where using Ben Wah Balls to tone your Pussy pays benefits. I moved his Cock about an inch into my Pussy, tightened down on him, then relaxed, then tightened again, then relaxed. I used my Pussy muscles to massage the head of his Cock while he drank in the vision, I had created… and he moaned… a lot.

I used my Pussy to play with him like this for a couple of minutes, and there was nothing he could do other than moan. I was on top, I was in control. Then I slowly slipped my Pussy down his Cock until he was all the way in me, and my Hot Spot pressed firmly against his Hilt. As my Venus Mons came into contact with his Hilt, I made my hip roll down, and without any encouragement, Tom made his hip roll up. This is how a girl's Hot Spot is massaged in Girl-On-Top. The girl has to fully complete her stroke, and both finish with a hip roll. He moaned again. So did I. For a woman to do a full stroke like that with a man is as nice for him as it is when he does it for you. He feels you use his Cock to open your Intro and he gets to watch as you slowly take him into you, all of him, every bit of Cock he has. He watches the Girl Show, and it's the best display of a naked woman that any man ever gets, but it's not just that. He watches you take his Cock into you farther and farther, he watches the rapture on your face as you feel his warm thickness fill you, over and over, all the way out, all the way in, as far into you as you can get him, because all the way in is where you want him. When the woman is on top, it's not about what he wants, it's about what she wants and what she wants is all of him she can get.

This is one of the neat things about Girl-On-Top for men, everything that's happening is something she is doing. She is putting on the show for him. She is taking his Cock as far into her as she can get it because that is where she wants it. A woman confirms a man's masculinity in a way that cannot be done as well, any other way.

We went like that for an hour. This is not the best position for him to have his orgasm, so whenever I felt it starting to build, I would slow down and just sit there for a few minutes and let it pass. After an hour while I had him fully in me, I leaned over and kissed him. "Please. Tom. Roll me over and finish," I asked.

He did.

He lifted me off of him laid me down on the bed, spread my legs wide, placed his Cock into my Intro and thrust all the way in. We had an orgasm together in less than a minute. It was glorious, my Pussy filled completely with his Cock, his hard short pumping strokes thrusting his Hilt into my Hot Spot. I was moaning so hard I was almost crying. After he finished, we both lay there together, breathlessly spent in the best way imaginable, him on top of me, his legs in between mine, my Pussy full of his Cock and his deliciously warm cum, his chest pressing down on my breasts as our breathing slowly returned to normal.

I kissed him. "Don't go," I suggested. "Let's just lay here like this."

He kissed me back. "For as long as you want," he agreed.

You can draw this out for a long time, and we did. The two of you are one, inside your own Love Bubble. Finally, I asked him, "Are you hungry?"

"Famished," he answered. "I've heard these Tikis have great crawfish." I knew for a fact they did, so we got up. I shrugged into my Coverup, and we headed over to the Bar. It was already seven thirty. He had low country style crawfish and grits. I had crawfish etouffee. Served with a bouquet of a lingering Afterglow.

Chapter Eight

The Tiki Bars are close to the Beach, and so are the bungalows. The easiest way back to my bungalow was right down the beach. There was a full moon out, so I stopped. I often do when the moon is full. I removed my bikini, placed it on my towel, and walked down to where the waves barely lapped my feet. I stood there nude with my hands out palms forward, looking up at heaven, drinking in the moonlight, and breathing deeply. This is a private moment with the Divine. Not just the Divine Feminine. I was drinking in the entire essence of creation and relishing all of it.

But as often happened, I was able feed both my soul and my Aphrodite Intuition this way. I used to think that Aphrodite communicating with women was unfair, particularly once I got good at understanding what people were thinking. This is a big advantage, and it would be helpful to so many women in so many ways. But I've come to feel this way: Testosterone makes men much stronger in many respects, why shouldn't estrogen and progesterone do the same for us?

For example, as I stood there, I realized that it was time for me to actually talk to Brian about what was going on, and I knew that the dark side of him that he'd been hiding was about to come to the front. Whatever it was, I knew I needed to be careful. Danger signs were flashing.

Aphrodite Intuition was telling me that he was part of this same Foundation for Righteousness group as the last guy, only a lot more capable, and there was more behind them than anyone of us had guessed at so far. This all became clear as I was looking up, relishing the heavens and basking in the soft gentle light of a silver moon. I tied my bikini back on and headed toward my bungalow. *"So,"* I thought to myself, *"Brian is part of the Foundation for Righteousness. This explains a lot. Does it mean he plans to try and kill me too? My intuition told me immediately the answer was... Yes!"* Well, I would be ready if or when he tried.

I walked up the path, thankful for the heads up from Aphrodite, and looked at my watch. It was about eight thirty which was a little earlier than normal. I'd have a little time to prepare for Brian. As I approached the door to my Bungalow, suddenly I stopped in my tracks.

Danger Close!

And the dangerous Aura belonged to Brian. No surprise there. Only this was not Aphrodite, but Zen.

Danger Close!

It was unmistakable. I realized that Brian was near my door on the right side where it would hide him when I opened it. So now I knew from two different sources, Aphrodite Intuition, and Zen. Yes, Brian did intend to kill me too.

Danger Close!

A lot of things suddenly became clear. Shannel had not achieved the third degree black belt. She was still completing the second degree, called Nan Dan, which means she didn't know much about sensing these things. Third Degree training is when you begin developing aura-sensing abilities. She would have simply walked in aware of the warning from Aphrodite to be careful, but unaware of the immediate danger, and the guy who killed her would have hit her in the head from behind with a club. She would never have seen it coming. This explained a lot.

Now I faced a dilemma. I could activate the silent alarm on my locket and just wait for Security to arrive. The problem was they would go in with guns drawn, and Brian would bite down on that pill. We would have eliminated the threat, but we would know nothing more.

We knew almost nothing about these people, not their location, or their numbers, their capabilities or intentions. We needed a lot more information and I knew it, plus Aphrodite was practically screaming it too … so no… I would have to try and handle Brian alone. I owed it to the memory of my friend.

Even though I was well trained, this was different. Doing the things we do in training was one thing, for real against someone who intended to kill you if you failed was another. This was the second time in a matter of days I faced a killer. Round one went to me, but Shannel's killer was not well trained. Now, once again, I was dealing with a man who intended to kill me. How much training had Brian received? Aphrodite made it clear it was a lot more than the other guy, but beyond that, I didn't know. I would be dealing with a man who had training, maybe a lot, was physically stronger than me, and armed. This was real, and as well trained as I was, there was always a risk, but here again, Aphrodite told me to believe in myself. This was a risk I did not have to take, but still, I knew what I needed to do. We needed information. All of those hours I'd spent under the night sky, drinking in the moonlight weren't for nothing. I would believe Aphrodite, follow her intuition, believe in myself, and take the risk to get the information. I did not activate my alarm.

The difference was, I knew Brian was there, and that was an advantage.

Was his location behind the door a problem? I thought this over for a second. Not really. Not since I knew he was there. Flukes happen all the time, and they can alter the outcome of these things, so there was a risk. But anything worthwhile has a risk, and this is why we train all the time, not just to handle the expected, but also the unexpected. I had to take the risk, and if things went south, find a way to deal with whatever came. But then I realized I could use Brian's own plan against him, and my own plan came together in my head.

I began singing a song I'd heard him playing on his MP3 so he would know I was coming and believe I was unaware of his presence.

Instead of just opening the door like I normally would, I suddenly pushed it open hard and as it reached him, I rammed my whole body into it, slamming it forcibly into his body with all of my strength behind it, knocking him reeling backwards and off balance. I backed off and dove headlong through the doorway, doing a forward twisting shoulder roll into the room. Since Brian was staggering backwards he never had a chance to swing his club. Even if he'd recovered from being hit by the door, the diving shoulder roll would put my body well under the arc of his swing. The shoulder roll took me about eight feet into the room, well out of range of whatever hand weapon he had, far enough away so I could easily defend myself if he reacted fast enough to attack, and the twist spun me around, so I was facing in the correct direction, looking him dead in the eye, exactly as I had planned, precisely as I had been trained.

But as Aphrodite had warned me, I was not the only one who was trained.

He immediately jumped at me with a flying kick taught at the First Degree Black Belt level, called Sho Dan. As he did, I realized he had both a club in his left hand and a Kevlar knife in the other. The jump he employed was one that would allow him to use the airborne kick to knock me down and then the lunge thrust with the knife. He could begin the thrust toward my chest while he was still in the air.

The extent of my training meant I realized all of this in an instant, and well before the kick could reach me, I did a back handspring to take me out of range of both the kick and the lunge thrust. All his knife cut was the air. As I came up to my feet, I looked at him and activated my alarm. "If you're going to kill me, Brian," I said calmly, "You're going to need to do a lot better than that." I knew projecting calm gave me an advantage. I might need it. Brian was clearly better trained than the other guy, at least Sho Dan, and dealing with two weapons can be about four times harder than dealing with one.

"You are a very pretty Heretic, an epic piece of ass, and deserve to die," he spat out vehemently and immediately did a Sho Dan level flying thrust at me again but this time Aphrodite warned me it was coming even before his body language gave it away and just as he jumped, I did a diving shoulder roll at a forty five degree angle away from the line of his jump. The problem with a flying thrust like Brian had done is you can't change your direction in the air. When he came down, I was behind him, off to his right, and in a much better position than he was. Just so you know, flying kicks are great for movies, and at certain times have advantages, but when you have to fight for your life it is better to keep your feet on the ground if you can.

Brian spun quickly to face me and began to raise the Billy Club, but I realized immediately the Club was a diversion. He was preparing to do another lunge thrust with the knife, camouflaging it by raising the club, but he had not made his move yet, so I still had a small window to take the initiative.

One of the keys to Martial Arts is to move faster than your adversary, and our training allows our decision making to be lightning fast. This is how we face a guy with a gun. We move! Very fast and not in a straight line, faster than they can accurately follow you and aim. But Brian did not have a gun. He had a club and a knife, and for that I needed to be closer. Before he could react again, I took two quick steps towards him and completely closed the distance between us. His eyebrows rose in surprise. The last thing he was expecting was for me to advance on him. Immediately, I performed a *"snap" sand-the-floor block* with my left hand and the focused snap of the back of my knuckles against the back of his hand broke several of the

135

bones there and knocked the knife free from his grip. It clattered across the floor out of his reach.

There was a grimace on his face from the pain. I took a step to my right, toward the club. As I did, I performed what is known as a *"snap" side punch* where your right forearm is coming up vertically, and you swing it hard to the right with a focused *"snap"* at the end.

This move "snapped" the back of my knuckles into the hand holding the club, breaking several bones in his other hand and knocking the club away as well.

It was time to end this. Before he could do anything else, I drove a *"snap" palm punch* into the center of his forehead with the heel of my hand which causes a serious concussion and knocks your assailant unconscious if performed properly.

My punch was performed properly. The threat was over.

Brian was down and unconscious, but at that point my Aphrodite Intuition raised another issue. That damn pill! We still needed information. I strode over to my nightstand quickly and grabbed the towel there. I rolled the end up, walked back over to him, pried his mouth open and shoved it down his throat as far as I could. When he came to, he would not be able to bite the cyanide pill if I could help it. I walked back over to the nightstand, picked up the lamp, and with one quick jerk, ripped out the electric cord. I went back over to Brian, rolled him onto his belly and bound his hands together behind his back with the cord, then rolled him back over onto his back. He'd be out for four or five minutes, I guessed, but after that he'd come to. At some point he'd be able to move, and who knew what could happen, so I walked over, and "snap" kicked him in the balls with my heel. Done correctly this will rupture at least one of his testicles.

My "snap" kick was correctly delivered.

I will admit it, stomping this man in the balls was extremely satisfying and I am not sorry. The last thing I am in life is a toy for the enjoyment of men. He was wearing a white G-String. It was beginning to redden on the side of his left testicle.

"Good," I thought to myself. He would not be able to walk for days.

The first security guard came running into the room. "Quick," I instructed, "go back to the infirmary, and get me a tranquilizer shot. Get back as fast as you can."

I looked at the other guard who came running in as the first ran out. "Help me get him into that chair," I said pointing to the wooden chair by my make-up table, "and let's retie his hands behind him." About a minute later, we had this done. Brian would not be able to get his hands free to remove the towel, and I had shoved it too far down his throat for him to spit it out. "Can you call your boss?" I said pointing to his radio.

"Already did. You're sure there is no one else here?" he asked.

"Yes," I answered definitively.

Several moments later, the first security guard returned with a nurse from the infirmary.

"Great," I said to the nurse, "we need to make sure he doesn't wake up for a while."

"Really?" he exclaimed.

"Really," I answered.

"OK," he said and gave him the shot.

Charley, the security chief arrived.

I quickly explained what had happened. "I think it might be a good idea for him to remove the pill," I suggested, pointing to the nurse. Charley agreed and gave the nurse his instructions. The nurse went back to the infirmary and returned with a medical bag. He found the pill in Brian's lip easily, numbed him and used a small scalpel to remove it.

"Mary Ellyn," the security chief said softly, "just so you know, this time we are not going to call in the police."

"Really?"

"No," he continued, "they weren't a lot of use the first time and would only be an interference this time. I am so proud of you for handling this so we could keep him alive."

I started to protest, but he held up his hand. "Stop, Mary Ellyn, and listen. Please, just listen to me. I know you didn't call us and took the risk so we could get information. I know you did. That was a terrific and brave decision in a really stressful situation. But the thing is, I can't do what I need to do with the police involved. I am not wasting your bravery by letting it get bottled up by a bureaucrat. To get the info we need, this cannot be done by the book. I want to interrogate him under the influence of drugs in twenty four hours. In the meanwhile, we will bring him in and out of consciousness every hour. This is actually how special forces do field interrogations. After a day, he will be so disoriented, he won't be able to keep from talking. It'll only take one dose of truth serum to break him."

"I see," I said softly as I considered this. I understood why he wanted to keep the police out of it but wondered why he was telling me.

"I'd like you to be there, if you are willing," he went on. "First, he's familiar with you. That helps the questioning. But that is not the only thing, you see, you were involved in the first attack, and now this one. The rest of the priestesses, priests, and most of the staff don't know, so we'd like to keep it that way... for now. Once a plan is in place we will let everyone know what is going on. Depending on what we learn, there may be something else you can do. We will never bring Shannel back, but we may be able to keep this from happening again."

"OK," I agreed.

I watched them put Brian on a stretcher and wheel him away. *This changes everything,* I thought to myself. I no longer was paired with anyone. It didn't surprise me when Helena knocked on my door a few minutes later.

"Are you all right, Mary Ellyn?" she asked.

"Physically, yes," I answered firmly. "You guys have trained us all very well. He never touched me. Mostly I am just emotionally shocked. Getting over that may take a while." I explained my conclusions about what had happened to Shannel, and why it had not happened to me.

"You know," I said as we talked and remembered the Intuition feelings I'd had on the beach, "it's possible there are some more of these people here. That was my sense of things from Aphrodite."

"Do you think so?" she asked.

"How would I know?" I answered with a shrug. "This was what my Aphrodite Intuition was telling me on the beach, so I'm just saying."

Helena knew all about Aphrodite Intuition and just nodded. "Why wouldn't they have attacked already?" she asked thoughtfully.

"Who knows," I answered. "I thought Brian and I were laying the groundwork for making *Eros* love. Clearly, I was wrong about that. I had warning bells going off the whole time, and I was careful, but we are not quitters here, so I kept trying. In the end, I was just a really nice piece of ass to him. If there are others, this will be true for them too. They won't be here for what we teach, but they are getting laid a lot. If there are others, maybe they want to prolong the fun as long as possible."

"Well, that's a good point," Helena said thoughtfully. "How do you feel about him using you for nothing more than sex?"

"I vacillate between vomiting and going over to the infirmary and snapping his neck." Helena nodded, and I continued, "I have the self-control not to do the second; the first is still up in the air."

"Well"—Helena chuckled—"if you're going to vomit into the air, please don't do it in my direction."

I laughed out loud. I couldn't help it, and this was good. It lightened the atmosphere and helped clear my head a little.

"I have an idea," I offered. "We could change the access so the guys can't get in by themselves like they do now. Only about a third of us are Sam Dan. We can sense danger and identify where it is coming from, but the other girls can't. If they walk into her bungalow together, and then the guy attacks, all of the girls here can handle the guy. All of us can. But if he's already inside, waiting in ambush, most of us can't."

Helena thought a minute. "I see your point. Everyone could just pick a meeting spot, and then go together to their bungalow." She nodded and then continued, "OK, we will do this, but we will have to reprogram our security systems. That's going to take a few days. Now, Mary Ellyn, after something like this we find it's good to stay occupied and you don't have a partner. Would you like to be the priestess doing the demo tomorrow? It's with Juan."

"Yes," I answered. "That's the one on advanced foreplay, right? One of the ones you usually do?"

"Yes,' she answered, "and yes. Are you sure?"

I looked at Helena, and decided I needed to go ahead and get this out. "Look, Helena, both of these guys used the word 'Heretic' for us," I began, "that means they are willing to kill us because they disagree with what we do. I realize that we practice an unconventional way of honoring God and the Divine Feminine, but that is our business. I don't care what they say or think; I believe what we do is beautiful, and it works. Lots of guys we trained have brought their wives here to get trained together, and we know their stories."

I continued without a pause. Once the flood starts, it's hard to stop.

"What we teach changes the men who come here. They are better lovers and connect to women both physically and emotionally on a much higher level than before they got here. They've made commitments, short term ones, but still commitments, and kept them, and they know how important the emotional connection is. They have felt it, lived it, and they leave here addicted to it. That means when they hook up with someone, they can actually be an excellent partner. What we do is good. Nobody on this Earth can convince me I'm wrong. We are not trying to force the way we think down anyone's throat, but if we let these people get to us, then they win."

I realized all of that came pouring out sort of like an outburst, so I paused and took a deep breath. "I'm sorry for the delivery, but not what I said," I continued in a softer tone.

Helena nodded in complete understanding but said nothing.

"I won't let that happen, Helena. I can't"—I looked up toward heaven—"otherwise Shannel was for nothing. So... I'm in... all in."

"Good for you, Mary Ellyn," she said. She paused to think for a moment and came to a conclusion. "Would you like some company tonight?"

"Very much," I said with a nod.

"Good. I'll send Juan over," she said and smiled, remembering that Juan was my first overnight instructor here.

"I'd like that too," I said softly, "If I could pick anyone, it would be Juan." She smiled broadly. "I know. I trust my intuition too. It's Aphrodite after all. We will get through this, Mary Ellyn," she offered supportively.

"I know," I agreed, looking her directly in the eyes, "and I want to help."

Chapter Nine

"*Right now, my emotions are a trainwreck*," I thought to myself. And if I had to be a trainwreck with someone, Juan would be the guy I'd choose. I knew this because when Helena said she was sending him over my heart leapt. It wasn't just because he was one of my first priests. We'd hooked up any number of times over the last couple of years at various of Fantasy Bay's attractions. We'd always gotten along well and had a lot of fun, but it was even more than that.

Any couple can use good foreplay technique to forge an emotional connection, but some are deeper than others, and some just naturally go really deep. Juan and I always had an especially deep *Eros* connection, probably the deepest I'd felt with anyone.

But how would he relate to me if I were a wreck? I didn't know. Dealing with an overwrought woman's emotions is not always pleasant for her girlfriends, and girlfriends are good at it. It is never pleasant for guys, and they normally aren't good at it. I knew Juan and my connection would be strong, but still, I wanted to try and get it together. The last thing I wanted was for him to think of me as a weepy eyed chick-i-poo, even though at the moment I felt like one. I did the best I could to calm down and get myself together.

***

Juan thought carefully as he approached Mary Ellyn's bungalow. The conversation he'd had with Helena had the potential to be transformative. At Fantasy Bay, the way they operated pretty much protected the priestesses and priests from forming attachments. Both knew that their Mon Chéri, or Ma Chérie would only be there two weeks. Not only that, but both members of the pair were also circulating and making *Eros* love with others for about eight hours a day, so fidelity was never part of the program. Attachments didn't happen.

What Helena was asking of him had the potential to change this. She'd asked him to focus on Mary Ellyn. The problem was that *Eros* love is addictive. All of the priestesses and priests knew it. When you focused your attention on one individual repeatedly, it was easy to find yourself in too deep to get out, and they called this Aphrodite's Man Trap. He had a good idea what would happen to his heart if he did. Helena was asking him to walk into Aphrodite's Man Trap with his eyes wide open. Was this a good thing? Was he ready for that? The truth was, he didn't know.

Mary Ellyn was clearly more than just "trained" in martial arts. There was a big difference between being "trained" and having the confidence and courage to voluntarily act on your training when your life was on the line if you failed. Reacting was one thing. This was so well trained as to be reflexive. She actually calmly thought it through and went forward anyway. He was a sixth degree Dan Master in Tae Kwon Do. He knew the difference.

Mary Ellyn's actions were not a reaction. She was not jumped or surprised. She chose to act alone, up against an armed man that intended to rape and kill her. She took the risk because it was the only way to take him alive.

What did that say about her? She was brave? Clearly. Committed? Without doubt. What else? Then he checked himself.

This wasn't something he could just "think through." He had to get out of his head and let his heart rule. The only questions were... what did Mary Ellyn need from him...? How could he be what she needed? Nothing else mattered right now. If that meant he got caught in Aphrodite's Man Trap, he'd just have to figure it out then. First up, heal this girl.

***

Juan knocked on my door a few minutes later. "May I come in?" he asked after I opened the door.

"Please, Juan," I replied, "Helena told me you would be coming."

He smiled, closed the door behind him, turned back to me, and before I could do anything to keep from it, my emotions took over and I collapsed into his arms, crying softly. This was not at all what I meant to happen, but I couldn't help it.

He enclosed me in his arms and held me with a gentle yet firm strength. He was so sweet, just holding me and letting me cry. In that moment I knew that Juan was the safest space I had ever known. After I had cried myself out, he took me lightly by the hand and led me over to the couch. He sat me down and began running his fingers through my hair and sat there looking at me with true tenderness in his eyes. He leaned over and kissed me with the softest, gentlest kiss I have ever experienced.

Dear God, I love it when a man has the sensitivity to know when a woman needs gentleness, and then the strength to be gentle for her.

"So," I said, "you know what's going on?"

"Yes," he answered. "Would you like to talk about it?"

I drew my breath in slowly, and then let it out. "Not really, Juan," I answered honestly. "I'm a wreck and you shouldn't have to deal with it."

"I know, Mary Ellyn," he agreed and softly, so gently, caressed my lips with his again. "I came knowing you would be a wreck," I could feel his strength, his kindness, and how much he cared as he kissed me and knew I had no need to be afraid of how he was going to feel. "How could you not be?" he continued, "Several nights ago your dear friend was killed. Then you confronted a trained killer, the guy who'd raped and killed her and tried to rape and then kill you. When he couldn't, he killed himself. Today, you took a risk for all of us. You chose to confront a second guy, another trained killer, who was going to rape and then kill you, and you took him down too. This takes a toll. Of course you're a wreck. It's why I wanted to come. Why I was glad Helena asked me."

This was new for me. I did not expect him to be glad he was here with me in the state I was in. This knowledge warmed me. Juan looked at me and continued, "Why don't you put your head here on my shoulder and we'll just fold you into my aura. We can just be quiet for a while, and I'll hold you."

The precise touch I needed. I nestled my head into his shoulder, and he wrapped me up in his arms. As he held me, I felt something I'd never known could happen. I felt Juan enclose me in his aura and his strength begin to flow into me. It was unlike any experience I'd ever had with a man.

It was not just his arms that wrapped me up. I was sheltered in his aura, which was tenderly healing me and giving me back my strength. At that moment I didn't know it, and it would be a few more days before I even began to realize what might be happening, but right then was when the first seed of *Agape* love with Juan was planted in my heart. What I did know was this man's gentle strength was helping me bring my emotions under control, and my strength back. I did not know a man could do something like that for a woman, but when they know how, they can. Juan did and it was beautiful.

After about a half hour Juan looked into my eyes with a gentle smile in his. "I know you're starting to feel better, but the other thing I know is you have to process all of this. We both know you need to talk to someone. I would love it so very much, Ma Chérie Amour, if you would talk to me."

I nodded slowly with a pleasant warmth glowing in my heart. This was not what I expected. He agreed to come over here, knowing I would be a mess. He came anyway, to help me. He knew I wasn't OK, so I didn't have to pretend to be OK with him. He accepted me in the condition I was in and gently gave me his strength, and tenderly soothed my heart. He called me Ma Chérie Amour which means "my sweet love." Those three words held life in them for me, and he knew it. He was not here just to make *Eros* love with me, which we both knew I needed, but to do something even more profound first. Before anything like that, he was here to give me back my strength and then heal my heart and soul. After he'd done that, we'd see about making *Eros* love. His priorities were in order. I'd had a lot of experience with men, but this was the first time I understood one of main things an *Agape* guy needed to be for his girl. Strong enough to be gentle enough with his girl so his strength could heal her when she needed it, and to know how to let her know there was nothing in the world more important to him. I didn't know about any of this because I'd never needed it before.

"Alright," I agreed looking at him looking back at me so tenderly. I took in a deep breath of his masculine essence and found I was able to relax a little.

I smiled and knew it was time to lighten things a little, "But we're going to need a drink, Mon Chéri Amour." I drew in another long breath and let it out. "Would you make us a Martini? There's some Hendrick's Gin open in the freezer."

Juan rose and made our drinks. He was not only trying to help, but he was so gentle with his words, he actually was helping. He was a Sixth Degree Dan Master and as tough as tough guys come. I knew he was a great and gifted lover, gentle, considerate, patient, controlled. I knew because I had experienced this with him any number of times, and every priest at Fantasy Bay was like this. But I expected the martial arts master in him would expect me to just brace up and muscle through everything. Instead, he was quite the opposite. I had never imagined he could be so gentle with me. I had not known that he could speak to me so tenderly. I had not realized he came to me to heal my heart and soul, to feed me with his strength, but that was clearly his purpose.

The realization brought tears to my eyes again, but this time for a different reason. My heart melted. It was one great thing to know how to make love with a woman, how to take her to the highest heaven. That ability is wonderful, and critically important to a relationship, but this was different, and I knew it was harder. Juan was a guy I could talk with about the hard stuff. As he sat back down and handed me my drink, I just snuggled into him and started to speak. It was natural, and the words came pouring out in a flood that lasted a long while.

Juan didn't correct me, or judge me, or evaluate what I did, or even try and tell me I did the right thing. He didn't try to "fix" anything. All he did was listen and encourage me to continue talking with him. When I finally finished, Juan went over to my fridge, made us another drink and got out some Havarti cheese for us to nibble on. What I still needed was his gentle touch. It was one very important thing to talk it through. This gets the poison out and heals the piece of your soul you damaged in the fight.

Did you know that anytime you fight, regardless of the outcome or reason, you damage a piece of your soul? It's true. No one ever wins a fight. Any time you have to use violence, physical, verbal, or any other kind, you damage an important piece of your soul. The reasons or goals behind your actions are irrelevant, even if they are necessary. You see, violence is addictive, no matter the reason for it. Zen has a philosophy for breaking the addiction and healing your soul after something like this happens, and this was what Juan had been doing with me, but afterwards your soul is still raw and to finish healing it needs to be soothed. Making a gentle version of *Eros* love was the perfect thing for that. Fortunately, this man knew all about what I needed, and how to do it well.

We sipped our drinks, nibbled the cheese, and Juan ran the fingers of his hand gently, lovingly, through my hair. When we finished, he stood, led me back to my bed, eased me onto my back, kissed me softly, and caressed me softly. He toyed with my nipples some, but not much, ran his finger up and down my Labia, and up into my G-spot a little, but with overwhelming gentleness, all the while either kissing me softly or looking into my eyes.

Exactly what I needed. I am a woman, a lover, a teacher of love, not a killer, or a hard ass, and I needed to feel like a lover, a teacher of love again. I had never before experienced the curative power of a man's gentle caress. First, most guys would not know how do something like that for a girl, and next, I'd never needed it before. Juan touched me like this for over an hour. No hurry, exceptional gentleness, complete kindness, overwhelming understanding.

Eventually, when I needed him to, he entered me, and we made slow gentle *Eros* love. Nothing special except the closeness I felt. Our auras melded into a Love Bubble quickly. Not long afterwards we were visited by two of Aphrodite's representatives, both a divine female and a divine male presence and I felt the overwhelming love of heaven. Unknown to either of us, the seed of *Agape* laying quietly in my heart was watered well and began to sprout. After his orgasm we laid entwined together and the warmth I felt had very little to do with the warmth of his cum. His warm Cock filled my Pussy, his Hilt pressed nicely into my Hot Spot, his gentle slow movements kept my orgasm going in that Afterglow Orgasm of *Eros* but it was the warmth of his soul that warmed me the most. We remained in our Love Bubble for a long time, but for the first time, for me at least, it seemed to be more than that.

When we pulled apart and later as we were falling asleep spooned with each other, I felt healed. I was no longer a wreck. I was whole again. And that was not quite all, in the hidden recesses of my heart something else was growing, but it was barely beneath my consciousness, and I was not aware of it yet.

The next morning, after martial arts practice, Juan and I made our way over to the demo theater. My focus had been lacking, but Juan had been really sweet about it, more like a friend and a partner than an instructor. I was going to need to process what this might mean, but it was not on my agenda at the moment.

The stage was sunken, theater style, with two hundred pairs of seats surrounding the front third of it. There were different camera angles around the room so everyone could see from every angle. I had sat out in the seats with a Mon Chéri many times, but never been on the stage before.

Juan walked and I sauntered onto the stage. I was dressed in a Little Red Dress, and Juan was in a Smoking Jacket. "Today's lesson," Juan began, "is about foreplay, but more advanced than what we talked about the first day. The first subject today is control. Even with a girl dressed like Mary Ellyn, you have to stay in control. Really good foreplay is slow and smooth. It has no breaks interrupting the emotional flow between you. This requires some advance planning. Something like a Smoking Jacket and G-string that can be easily untied is great for men."

"For women," I took over and continued, "It's a bit more complicated. Imagine that!" I said with a chuckle. "Girls, you need a dress that comes off easily, either over your head, or one that slips off and falls easily to the floor. Neither of you need to be fumbling around with clothing. It interrupts the rhythm of your foreplay. You don't need a bra so don't wear one. If you're going to wear panties at all, you need the ones that untie at the sides. Some guy's love playing with a girl's panties, so if you know your guy likes this, wear them, but if you don't know, don't bother. Same with stockings."

"How a girl dresses for *Eros* love is not about her, it's about him and what he likes. If he likes playing with stockings, wear them, but you also need to wear a garter belt because stockings have a bad history of not staying up when a girl is in the throes of passion. If he likes playing with panties, wear the ties ones and tie them over your garters so the panty strings don't get tangled up when they are being taken off. Normally you should plan on the stockings and garter belt staying on as you make love.

There is just no good way to get them off without interrupting your flow, and you don't need them to be off."

Juan spoke up again, "Even more importantly, we want to reiterate what we said the other day. Good foreplay is slow. The single most important key is this. Take your time. This communicates to a woman that what she wants... from... you, is the most important thing... for... you. You don't tell her with words, you show her with actions."

We both moved into the lesson from there. Once we were finished and off of the stage, I looked at Juan. "Would you like to go over to the Rain Forest Park?" I suggested, "We could have lunch over there and go on one of the walks."

"I was desperately hoping, you would ask," he answered and took my hand. For the first time in several days, I felt lighthearted and free.

***

As Mary Ellyn and I left the stage and went back to the dressing room, I knew, for me at least, this was coming to a tipping point, a place where I was too far in to unravel our lives. And I still didn't know what I wanted to do. Go forward with this wonderful girl, or not? I had no idea what she wanted. Would she change up her whole life for me or not? Our emotional connection was unreal, no denying it, and I was sure she wouldn't deny it either. But the problem was coming up that happens to all relationships. They start out so wonderful they are unreal and after a while they have to transition to real. Those that last manage to bring the magic with them into reality. Could I? Could she? Did I want to? Did she want to? If I was going to call this off and unravel it, this was going to need to happen soon or I wouldn't be able to. And then I felt my heart talking to my head. "Just go with it Juan. You've been preparing for this girl your whole life. Put this in her hands. Trust her. You know how. She knows how. *Eros* love has taught you both."

Chapter Ten

We made our way over to the Jungle Café and had crawfish almondiné for lunch. After lunch, I took Juan by the hand, and we headed to nature trail number three. There are five, and like many things at Fantasy Bay, these each have their own twist. All five are designed for a uniquely sensual Rain Forest experience. There are a great many nature trails in the Rain Forest of Central America, but most are not designed for making love. These are.

The Panamanian Rain Forest is a truly wonderful paradise of tropical foliage, palms, hibiscus, hyacinth, bromeliads, orchids, bougainvillea, tigerwood, Brazilian cherry, and other varieties too numerous to name. There are colorful birds of paradise, macaws, cockatoos, and toucans.

Each path is native gravel and makes a loop winding around through the rain forest. On this particular trail, there were occasional off-shoot paths that go back about twenty yards to benches. Just past the bench is a clear water pool.

As we prepared to start down the trail, we faced each other. I kissed him and untied and removed his G-string as he took off my top and bottom. We looked into each other's eyes, cleared our minds of everything, and let *Eros* love enfold us. We soon found ourselves in our own Love Bubble, turned, joined hands, and headed down the trail.

For couples who can create a Love Bubble there is a level of joy available in the Rain Forest that is beyond anything else I have ever experienced, even more than the Air Bell. Here were we; two people walking down the trail, completely naked in a glorious space, enveloped in our own little piece of Heaven. Being naked in a place of natural beauty has nothing to do with sexuality. It's about two individuals becoming a single 'self' and then this 'self' becoming one with nature itself, and when this occurs something transformative begins to happen.

As you start down the trail, the air itself seems alive, and the simple act of breathing deeply, in through your nose, out through your mouth, fills you with incomprehensible wonder as the aromas of the tropical foliage titillates your nostrils.

As you move a little farther, the colors shine brighter, the aromas become more vivid, the bird calls more vibrant. Every living thing seems to resonate at a higher level.

As you walk naked with a lover down such a trail in such a place, you soon discover the Spirit of the Rain Forest has joined your Love Bubble and with just the acts of looking around, walking hand in hand, and breathing; you are making *Eros* love with nature itself. When the couple maintains this relationship with the spirit of the Rain Forest, and adds in making *Eros* love with each other, the combination creates an experience that verges on the infinite.

When we were about two thirds of the way down the trail, we came to an offshoot path. We had passed several.

We looked into each other's eyes, wordlessly nodded and turned down the path.

It led to a Cherry bench. The bark had been meticulously stripped and the underlying wood painstakingly polished. Juan took me in his arms and kissed me softly, and then backed me against the bench. I eased my butt up onto the bench, leaned back and spread my legs wide. He did not stroke me with his hands. He used his Cock, moving it back and forth along my Labia. He took a breast in each hand and massaged them gently with his hands, moving the nipple against his chest, while kissing me softly.

This is another form of advanced foreplay. It can only be done standing up. It engages every part of a woman, every part of a man, simultaneously. When you add in the sensations of making love with the Spirit of the Forest, you are ensconced in an envelope of existential sensations unknown in any other space.

Juan and I were in this envelope for a time that could not be measured. Time has no meaning in such a place. Two people, one with each other, one with nature, surrounded by the lush tropical environment in all of its splendor, transcends anything that connects you to time or even life, apart from the wonder of that moment.

Finally, somehow, I knew it was time. I looked into Juan's eyes and nodded. He smiled but said nothing.

We joined hands again, they just seemed to come together without conscious thought, walked down to the pool maintaining the connection we felt to nature and to each other and then wadded slowly into the pool. The water was clear and warm, and the foliage and flowers were spectacular. At the other end was a submerged reclining padded lounge.

I turned, slowly, sensuously straddled it, sat down, and lay back, spreading my legs wide. The water was lapping my breasts. Juan placed his knees between my legs, placed his Cock at the top of my Venus Mons, then ran it down to the Intro and I felt his wonderful thick warmness fill me with one grand decadently slow thrust.

He pulled out a couple of inches and thrust in again until his Hilt pressed firmly into my Hot Spot. Then out a couple of inches, and slowly back all the way in again, with a firm finish. Out a couple of inches, and slowly back in again, firm finish. Out a couple of inches, and slowly back in again, firm finish, all the while the lower two-thirds of our bodies submerged in the warm pool waters.

We were making *Eros* love with each other and with the Rain Forest which encompassed us. I couldn't tell what parts of us were him or me or where we ended, and the forest began. A macaw flew by, and it seemed like I could feel the wind flow through her wings. Juan, me, the Rain Forest foliage and fauna, everything melded into one. Nothing more beautiful ever happens to people in this world.

We finally pulled apart, returned reluctantly to the trail and strolled slowly out of the Rain Forest ensconced in the existential effervescence we had created with the Spirit of the Rain Forest itself, and headed back to my bungalow. Looking back on it, something began to change for me in that pool.

Perhaps it was the roller coaster of emotions I'd been through. Perhaps it was that I had given Juan a piece of my heart on my first day at Fantasy Bay, and it had stayed there like a seed and the waters of the pool brought it into bloom. Perhaps Juan and I had made true *Eros* love together a number of times with practically no interruption to break our emotional flow, and my heart just took over.

Perhaps it was the essence of being one, not only with Juan but also with the Rain Forest itself, and when you share something so profound with another human being, you are forever bound.

More likely the changes I felt were the totality of all of this. Were these feelings real *Agape* love? That was the first question. Was Juan feeling it too? This was the second. How would he react? That was the third. I didn't know the answers and that was the unsettling part; you feel these wonderful feelings in your heart, but you don't yet know if they are shared.

It's like this for at least one of the partners in almost all relationships that grow into the *Agape* phase. Few couples have both partners arrive at *Agape* in the same moment of time. You don't know how your partner is feeling and want to give them space, and not push it. At the same time, you know how you are starting to feel, it's too wonderful for words, and you want to push it. It seems so easy to make a stupid mistake, and the conundrum makes you feel vulnerable.

All I knew for certain was our relationship was evolving. It was another day before I fully sorted out the first question. It was there in that pool, in that incredibly beautiful tropical place, that I began falling completely in

Eros + *Agape* love with Juan. Not the kind of sensual *Eros* love we teach at Fantasy Bay, but what that sensual love is intended by Aphrodite to evolve into, the combination of *Eros* and *Agape* love. My next question was Juan. How did he feel?

If he fell in *Agape* love with me, it would mean changes for us both. *Agape* love only survives in an environment of fidelity. Was he ready for us to go *Agape*? Just supposing he was, what about the changes that would bring? Was he ready for those? He'd been making *Eros* love with three girls a day, sometimes more, for several years. How could he possibly be ready to give that up for me? This was probably the most unsettling part. Would he view a permanent *Eros* + *Agape* relationship with me to be of greater value than what he had going on?

I knew I had to leave this in Aphrodite's hands, but when you truly understand the Divine Feminine, this is not as innocent as it may sound. Aphrodite encourages a girl to make *Eros* love with her guy… a lot. Every chance you get in fact. She wants the reality of you to become beyond his wildest erotic dreams. She wants you to let the reality of him become beyond yours. Before long neither of you can imagine anything other than a life together. *Eros* love, given a little time, becomes an exquisite trap worthy of a Goddess.

That's the truth!

I knew this, but then so did Juan. He would know he needed to put on the brakes if he didn't want this. He'd know he needed to do it soon, before it went too far. The problem was, I was already too far gone to come through this with my emotions intact. I was incapable of stopping the 'us' we were becoming if I did want to, and I didn't want to. Would he want to stop? If he did, it would be a bloody broken heart for me. But if he wanted us to go forward, it would be the best thing that could happen. Where was he? Time would tell. I decided I would not listen to my fears, and I would give him time.

We went back to the café and had dinner. As we were walking back toward my bungalow, we looked at each other, and wordlessly understood that we would spend the rest of the evening together. I took comfort in that. Juan could have any girl he wanted. On this night, the only girl he wanted was me and this knowledge warmed the cold stomach pit where fear grows.

We watched the sun slowly set into the Pacific and as it sank below the horizon, I silently thanked the Goddess for Helena. She knew exactly what she was doing when she sent Juan to me. I believe her Aphrodite Intuition told her exactly what should grow between us, but the question remained. Where was Juan's heart? Would he trade the life every young man dreams of, for me?

Chapter Eleven

Juan and I rose the next morning, the day of the interrogation. As I got out of bed, I turned and faced him. I slowly, seductively pulled my camisole up over my head, shook my hair out with a flip, untied and removed my bra, then untied my panties and placed my left knee coquettishly on the bed. The suggestion was wordless but could not have been louder if it had been a shout.

As I stretched before him, Juan smiled and his Cock became erect immediately. He stretched to, and the muscles in his ripped chest rippled, his shoulder and arm muscles flexed, and as his Cock stood up like a flagpole, I felt a familiar tug in my Pussy.

He was beautiful, and every girl I've ever known loves it when her guy puts on a show just for her, I certainly did.

"Let's brush our teeth, and go to the shower," he suggested. Once we were there, he positioned me on the seat with the warm shower water cascading delightfully down upon us.

He kissed my lips, then my nipples, then went down on his knees, spread my legs, and kissed my Intro, rubbing his nose into the top of my Venus Mons and started licking my Hot Spot.

He ate my Pussy right there in that shower for about a half an hour, licking my Hot Spot, fingering my G-spot with one hand, fingering my taint and ass with the other while warm water sprayed softly over us, then with no warning, he stood up, and with one firm, strong, slow thrust, drove his thick, warm Cock all the way into me and we went over the moon together.

Needless to say, Juan had his orgasm deep in me, and the timeless wonder of those short delicious thrusts were only enhanced by the warm water cascading down upon us. I began to realize there was a new hope developing in my heart. It centered around Juan, but I could not yet dare to believe. The changes to our lives would be profound. Was he ready? Was I ready? How would I know?

We got dressed and walked over to the building where the interrogation was to be held. Brian was in the next room. We could see him seated in a chair through a large one way mirror. His eyes looked vacant.

Charley looked at me. "We've had him knocked out for two hours, awake for two hours, out for two, back and forth for the last day," he began. "He's been awake for about an hour. As expected, he's totally disoriented. We injected a truth serum, scopolamine, about thirty minutes ago."

Helena looked at me. "Your voice is one he's familiar with," she said quietly, "and he knows you. We believe it will be best if you ask the questions. The rest of us will watch from here." She handed me a sheet of questions.

Charly added, "He is not handcuffed, but we'll be right here if you need us."

"I won't need you," I replied. There are times in life when you just know something. Aphrodite Intuition is a

164

good example, but this was different. This was Zen. Once we had what we needed, if this man gave me a pinch of manure, I'd snatch his windpipe right out of his neck and dance on his frigging grave. I knew it. Crossing me was a death sentence for him. He'd know it too. Such is the nature of Zen.

Charley nodded. "OK. Just use a normal even tone of voice. We have him wired to a lie detector. His answers will normally be short. It is likely he will pass out at some point. The most important piece of information is their address."

"And whether their computers are networked," Helena added. "This is crucial to a plan we have in mind. Hopefully they are. Here's an earpiece so we can talk to you. We will let you know once we have a baseline. Don't go to Part Two until we tell you."

I put the earpiece into my ear, walked into the room and sat in the chair in front of Brian. I saw a small sign of recognition on his face.

The first questions to people hooked to a lie detector are always about things you already know the answer to. It establishes the baselines for distinguishing between the truth and a lie.

After I sat there for a minute, I asked the first question. "Where have you been for the last several days?"

"Fantasy Bay," he answered thickly.

"What were you doing there?"

"Screwing really pretty girls, like you." I despise guys like this.

"Was it fun?"

There was a pause, like he didn't want to admit the answer. "Yes."

"Was it your intention to rape and kill me from the beginning?"

"Yes."

"Why did you wait?" We were approaching Part two.

"To have fun with you first."

"Mary Ellyn," I heard Helena say in the earpiece, "we have a good baseline."

I started into Part two. "What is your name?"

"Brian Calhoun." The slow thick character to his voice was not improving.

"Where do you live?"

"Silver Trout Springs, Arkansas."

"What is your address?"

"427 3rd Street."

"What is your phone number?"

"777-898-8989."

"Who sent you to Fantasy Bay?"

There was a brief pause, as if he were struggling not to answer, but only a brief one. "The Foundation for Righteousness."

"Where are they located?"

Again, a pause, this time a bit longer. It was clear he did not want to answer. The disorientation added to the scopolamine was clearly not giving him any choice. "Box 87, Rural Route 3, Silver Trout Springs, Arkansas." The sluggishness in his voice seemed to be increasing.

"Do you use computers?"

"Yes."

"Are they networked?"

"Yes."

"How many of you did they send?"

"Six."

"What are their names?"

"I don't know."

"What did they send you to do?"

Another pause, longer. "To kill heretics like you."

"For what purpose?"

"To send a message that your sinfulness and false doctrine will not be tolerated." There was no pause there at all. The answer flowed out smoothly, almost like a mantra that had been repeated many times.

"How many members does the Foundation have?"

"One-hundred and thirty-seven."

"Who is your leader?"

The longest pause yet. Finally, he replied, "The Reverend Doctor Billy John Buxton."

OK, that was good. We had all we truly needed at this point. Even so, I continued on the list I'd been given. "What do you believe is the main heresy at Fantasy Bay?"

"Teaching that there is a Goddess."

"Are there any other heresies?"

"Encouraging young women use their body out of wedlock, and the failure of women to acknowledge the authority of men over them."

"What is God's purpose for women?"

"To bear and raise children and serve the needs of men."

"Nothing more?"

"No."

There were more questions, but Brian passed out at that point. As two orderlies came to take him away, I rejoined the others in the adjoining room.

"Well done, Mary Ellyn," Juan congratulated me.

"Yes," Helena agreed as everyone nodded.

"We will try and get more info from him in a few hours, but we have what we need," Charley said in summary.

I looked at Charley. "If it's OK, I would prefer not to be involved in the next round."

Helena studied me for a second. "Why, Mary Ellyn?"

"Now that we have what we need, I will be tempted to kill him if I ever see him again," I answered in a firm clear voice. "I won't, but it would be a struggle, and he is not worth the effort it would take for me not to kill him."

"I understand," Helena replied with a nod.

I looked from Charley to Helena. "Do you have a plan?"

"Yes," Helena answered with a firm nod. "At least Phase One of a plan. We are going to send two people up there and infect their computer network with a background virus that allows us to access their hard drive."

"It'll provide us complete access to everything on their hard drive, including their member list," Charley continued, "as well as their plans. We will know if there are any more of them here now, and anyone from their organization who signs up to come here in the future will be apprehended before they ever arrive. To do this, we have to penetrate their facility and put a memory stick into one of their computers for a few minutes without being discovered."

I nodded.

This made sense. It would end the threat. "What will you do with Brian?"

"Do you really want to know?" Helena asked gently.

"Yes," I answered simply.

"Brian, as you know, had a cyanide pill. He was willing to die for this cause," Helena began.

"So, we are just going to kill him?" I asked, not quite believing what I assumed she meant. Even though I might really want to, I knew I would not.

"No, of course not," Helena answered immediately. "But we will not turn him loose either. We'll take him to a part of Brazil deep in the Amazon inhabited by the Tupi tribe. They practice cannibalism on outsiders who they catch in their territory without permission. We will maroon him, naked, alone, no shoes or tools. Because of your wonderful kick to his nuts, he will have a hard time walking for quite a while so it will be almost impossible for him to avoid the Tupi, but if he does and if his survival skills are excellent, he will have some chance to survive."

"If not, the Tupi will be nice to him at first. They are a closed society and have an instinctive knowledge that they need some diversity in their gene pool. They will breed him like a horse to several of their women as they fatten him up. Then they will kill him, clean him like a hunter cleans an animal, spit him and roast him over a fire like the pig he is. He will at least do one useful thing; provide the Tupi with a feast. At the very least he will have the chance to make peace with God before he dies."

I nodded slowly. This seemed fair. Especially the idea that he could become food for cannibals. I could think of no other good use for Brian. In my view, such should be the end of anyone who would rape and murder a woman. Those Tupi's are people after all and they do have to eat something, it might just as well be him.

I nodded, "Who will you send to Arkansas?"

"We hoped you and Juan would like to go," Helena answered looking at me directly.

My answer was crisp and immediate. "There is nothing I would like better."

"Juan?" she inquired.

He looked at me and smiled, "Me too."

Helena smiled broadly, looked over at me and winked. She knew exactly what this meant and knew I did too. "I'll make the travel arrangements then

Chapter Twelve

Later that day, Juan and I were on the first flight to Houston. There were no direct flights to Little Rock from Panama City, so we had to change planes. Once in Little Rock, we would pick up a car and drive to our hotel. There was only a small 1960s-style hotel in Silver Trout Springs, and Charley felt that would be too conspicuous. We had been booked into a Wyndham in Hot Springs, about thirty minutes on the other side.

One way to get to Hot Springs would take us through the town of Silver Trout Springs itself. A small detour would take us right by the 'Foundation for Righteousness' facility. We would have an opportunity to get a good look at conditions on the ground and see if they differed from what we had seen on Google Earth. If plans needed to be changed, we would be able to change them at that point.

I drove while Juan studied the map, and we wound through the delightful Ozark countryside on a fairly well-traveled two-lane road. The spring peace lilies were blooming wild everywhere. I'd never seen so many before. This was not a Rain Forest, but was lush in its own way, delightful old growth trees were everywhere.

As we drove, I wondered if we could achieve the oneness with this forest that we'd done with our Rain Forest. That was an interesting question, and it would be fun to find out if we had the time. Our directions indicated that about a mile and a half on the other side of Silver

Trout, a road named MacArthur Park went off to the left. The Foundation for Righteousness' facility was supposed to be down that road, about two miles.

We passed through Silver Trout Springs, a pleasant little Ozark town, and came to MacArthur Park Road. Charley had instructed us to make sure we were not being followed. Juan was checking carefully, but there was only a Borden's Milk semi behind us, and nothing behind the truck.

MacArthur Park was coming up. "Anyone back there?" I asked.

"No one other than the semi," Juan replied. "After you make the turn, why don't you slow down, and we'll see if anyone follows."

I made the turn, slowed down and no one followed. We were in the clear.

The entire area was wooded, with a forest clearly intended for clear-cut logging. We could tell because the trees were growing in straight line rows, and the underbrush was kept fairly clear so the soil's nutrients could be devoted to tree growth. I remember thinking it was a pretty ugly forest as forests go. There is something weird about a forest with all of the trees about the same age and all growing in straight lines, like corn in a corn field. Natural forests are not like this. Somehow it did not seem possible to make love with nature here. A few moments later, I could see the site we were looking for up ahead.

The first building appeared to be a parsonage, which had two cars parked in its driveway. The center building was a Church. There was a sign out front announcing:

Foundation for Righteousness
The Reverend Doctor Billy John Buxton
Services
Sunday – 8:30AM 10:00AM 7:00PM
Wednesday 7:00PM

We were in the right place. On the far side was a Recreation Hall, and what we thought would be their offices. As we drove past the church, I could clearly see this was the case. I pointed, "Looks like a dining hall up front, and offices in the back."

"Yeah," Juan agreed but we needed some answers to know how to proceed.

Was there an alarm system?

What kind?

What kind of locks?

We had three potential plans depending on what we found. Plan A was the easiest one. We had been given a standard lock-picking machine that locksmiths have. You attach it to the door with suction, and it picks the lock for you. The problem was it only works with keyed locks.

Plan B was if the lock was not keyed but had numbers that you punched in. We had two tiny trail cameras with us. From our study of the building on Google Earth, we knew there was a row of shrubbery in a planter across the front entry. We could plant the cameras and then wait in our hotel for someone to come and punch in the Code. This was probably the riskiest because we would have to spend more time in front of the door placing the cameras, and we would be visible from the road.

If the lock was electronic, it meant Plan C, which was to remove the glass from a window in the back and go in there. This would require the most total time, but we would be out of sight. Out of sight was good, but the time it might take was not.

The problem at the moment was that there were a number of cars in the parking lot, and I knew the last thing we needed was to attract any attention.

"Shall we come back tomorrow?" I suggested.

Juan nodded. "Saturday is not likely to be a workday, so, I think that's best."

We drove on to Hot Springs and checked into our hotel.

That night after a pleasant country style catfish dinner, we had barely gotten back to our room when Juan's cell phone rang. "Hi, Helena," Juan said pleasantly and then began to listen intently with a look of concern playing out across his face. "What?" he said with a shocked tone. "Wait, I'll put you on speaker."

"Can you both hear us?" Helena asked.

"Yes," I answered.

"There's been another attack," Helena explained. "We have no details yet. I'm going to check it out now, but we'll let you know if there is anything that affects you. If you don't hear from us proceed as planned."

The next morning, Juan and I headed out early. Even if there were people working, they might sleep in on a Saturday and get in a little later. Our idea was to get there at sunrise and be gone well before eight a.m.

Once we parked in front of the office, Juan put our map on his lap. This way if someone from the church approached us, we could claim I had taken a wrong turn, and we were lost.

No one was around, so we got a good look at everything. The windows were clean but not upgraded. They had large glass panes of the sort which old offices of that era often had, plenty large enough for us to climb through.

"The windows are big enough." I observed.

"Yes," Juan agreed, "and there is no alarm system." This made sense because the response time to get all of the way out here would be too long for an alarm system to do any good.

I looked at the door carefully. It was an electronic lock.

Juan and I looked at each other. "Electronic. Plan C," he noted.

I nodded slowly, "tonight?" I could feel my Aphrodite Intuition letting me know this was not going to be as easy as we had hoped.

"Right," Juan agreed with a single firm nod of resolve. "Let's check out that logging road."

The forest on the far side was the same clear-cut timber operation with very little undergrowth. We looked around as I pulled back out on MacArthur Park. No one pulled in behind us. These people were clearly not expecting unwanted visitors.

We drove about five hundred years farther, found the logging road and turned into it. We drove down about a hundred yards and around a shallow curve.

"Good," Juan announced, "our car can't be seen from the road."

"So, that's everything on our list." I nodded.

By the time we got back to our hotel it was about ten-thirty in the morning and we had time to kill. We looked at the brochures, and I found one advertising private hot spring grottos. Normally a person should not stay in a hot spring for more than fifteen minutes if the water is hotter than 120 degrees, but these people cooled off the hot mineral water to about a hundred degrees so it wasn't really hot. More like warm, and a "couple could enjoy the waters indefinitely," according to the brochure. I showed it to Juan and arched my eyebrows inquisitively. He smiled wordlessly, took my hand and we were on our way.

The spring rose in the deep bowels of the mountains and then formed what geologists call a "plume" which conveyed the water to the outside. This plume was a great deal larger than needed to carry the current water volume, so a steel walkway had been built going back to the spring. In the 1950's, someone had carved these underground grottos back into the granite along the walkway. The grottos were private and fed by the hot spring, but the waters were arranged in a fashion to form a waterfall, which was both attractive, and cooled off the water.

Perfect for a couple to make love in. Juan and I found ours and shed our clothes.

We began our time in the grotto with an embrace, two naked lovers intimately intertwined. This a wonderful form of prelude to foreplay for a woman when it's practical. Your nipples being tickled by his chest hair, your Labia being nuzzled by his Cock, your ass being massaged by your man. It certainly qualifies as foreplay in its own right, but we place such a high priority on foreplay, that most of the time it's a really nice way to start.

Around the sides were carved seats, in the center was a carved chair. We wadded into the warm mineral water, inhaling the aromatic vapors. It's said these vapors have healing properties, but I know little about any of that. Juan sat on the chair and I straddled his legs and positioned his Cock in my Groove, and leaned into him so his chest hair was tickling my nipples again.

I suppose this position would technically be considered seated Girl-On-Top, but technicalities like that meant nothing to Juan and me. I moved back and forth slowly, massaging my Hot Spot with his Cock while I kissed him. Actually. I like this position better than the traditional Girl-On-Top, because we can still kiss, and it's a lot easier to maintain an emotional connection when you can kiss.

After we'd made out for a few minutes, I eased Juan's Cock into my Pussy, and I felt him slowly open me, pass my Intro, then my G Spot, engage my Cervix, slowly and completely stretch me out and then he massaged my Hot Spot with his Hilt. In the warm mineral water environment of the hot spring, it's normal if you just felt a little lazy, so we were in no hurry. Juan eased me up until he was almost out and then I let gravity slowly take me back down, using my thighs to control the speed of my descent as I felt his warmth fill me deeper and deeper until there was no more of him to take. These are wonderful sensations for a girl if she does this slowly. He eased me up and I slowly eased back down, over and over, kissing all the while. When he had his orgasm we shared it like we always did, and then we shared the Afterglow Orgasm, nicely enhanced by the warm spring waters and their mineral vapors for over an hour.

"The heat and the mineral water are really nice," Juan concluded.

"Yeah," I agreed, "but I still like the tropics a lot better."

We went on to our hotel, checked in and texted Helena and Charley, told them the situation, and our intention to try and get in tonight.

"*Good Luck,*" they both texted back although we all knew if we needed luck, this meant a problem. The best thing was easy in, easy out and vanish.

There was only one thing we didn't know. Did the Foundation have a night watchman? We assumed they did. My Aphrodite Intuition told me they did, and that we needed to be prepared, so the worst case was the way to bet. We were prepared one way or the other. I knew Juan was hoping everything would go smoothly. I knew better. Aphrodite's Intuition told me plainly it would not be that simple, and I decided to tell him.

"Mon Cheri Amour, Aphrodite seems to be telling me it's not going to be that easy," I said with a sober tone, "There is a watchman, and he will interrupt us."

Juan looked at me and nodded. He was quite familiar with our intuition, but no priestess at Fantasy Bay had ever needed to use it in a situation like this before. "Well, we're ready if that's the way it goes."

We went to a rib place and had dinner while we waited for the sun to set. I will tell you one thing. I don't know much about Arkansas, but they do good ribs in Hot Springs. We went back to our hotel and changed into black outfits. The sun was well set, so it was time.

"Ready?" Juan asked casually as if we were going out for an evening stroll.

"Let's go," I answered as cheerfully as possible, and we drove back to Silver Trout Springs.

Once we passed the Foundation's site, I drove to the logging road, turned and drove in a couple hundred yards past the curve. No one driving by would ever see our car. Our first instruction was to sit tight for ten minutes and let our vision fully adjust to the night.

After the adjustment period, we got our tool bag and walked through the forest to an area close to the back of the offices. Picking our way through the limited undergrowth was not particularly hard, and we paused at the forest's edge.

We could see headlights coming down MacArthur Park, and waited to see what would happen. There were two cars, but they passed without slowing.

"Ready?" I asked, once I was sure there were no headlights coming in either direction.

"As I will ever be," Juan answered.

We jogged across the open space quickly, but once we were up to the back side of the building, there was no chance of us being seen from MacArthur Park. There were several windows along the back with the large panes. I selected a window and shined a flashlight in, while Juan took out the chisel.

"What about this one?" I pointed. "It's an office with a computer, but I can't tell anything else."

"One is as good as another," Juan guessed and chiseled out the caulk that held the windowpane in. Next was to attach a suction device that would let us pull the glass out without breaking it. Once this was done, he set the glass down carefully about ten feet away from the window we were using. Part of Plan C was for us to replace and recalk the window. We didn't want to break the glass by accident.

"Here," he said, "let me give you a boost."

Seconds later, I was inside. As I had thought, this was an office of some kind, and I began looking at the computer. Juan would stay outside in case there was a night watchman who patrolled the grounds first. My intuition was not suggesting this was the case. Everything felt clear.

"Good," I thought to myself noticing the thumb drive port on the computer. I quickly inserted the memory stick and pushed the small activation button on the side. A tiny red light came on. Hacking into a computer system from

the outside, with all of the firewalls and security measures, was one thing. Inserting the right kind of background program loaded on a memory stick from the inside was easy. Once active it would allow us to copy the hard drive remotely from Charley's office at Fantasy Bay, and remote connect any time we wanted to. It was going to take seven minutes to download the program, but once the download was complete, I could just take the memory stick and climb back out. We would replace the glass and leave. Easy. The only interruption might be a night watchman, but I knew he was coming. I just knew it. My Aphrodite Intuition expected him any minute.

"He could be here any minute, Juan," I warned softly. I was aimlessly looking out the window, killing time, waiting for the download to finish, when I noticed headlights shining through the parking lot. This meant someone was pulling in. It could only be a night watchman. Once again, I was right.

"OK," I thought to myself. *"It's go time."*

"Mary Ellyn," Juan said softly as he vaulted up into the room and dropped into a crouch behind the desk, "go back into that alcove, behind the door." There was no closet in this office, but there was an alcove behind the door. Maybe the guy would just open the door, shine his light in and go on.

Maybe… but I knew Aphrodite didn't think so. In fact, I had the feeling the man would become a threat to Juan. The only thing we could do was to be prepared. I would be out of his direct line of sight. So would Juan. Maybe he would not notice the pane of glass missing. It depended on how seriously he took his job. I moved over to the alcove as I heard the front door open. Seconds later, we heard steps coming down the hallway. They would stop, a door would open, then close a few seconds later, then more steps. I was feeling no particular danger from the night watchman's aura, but my intuition was still telling me I would have to handle this.

The man was approaching the door to the office we were in. Seconds later, the door opened. Suddenly:

Danger Close!

I sensed the change in the man's aura. A few seconds later, a light flashed around the room.

Danger Close!

"Go on," I thought to myself. *"Just go on,"* but deep inside I was sure he would not, and more, I knew he would try and kill Juan.

Danger Close!

Then the steps came into the office. "I have a sensitive nose. I could smell your cologne," a voice with an Arkansas drawl announced as he trained the light into my eyes and pointed his revolver at me. Priestesses wear perfume all the time, its fragrance never really leaves any woman that does.

"A girl!" he exclaimed. "Oh, I see. You must be one of those Heretics. Still, I'd never have thought they'd send a girl for a man's job. So, you are on to us. That means one of our guys will not be coming home I suppose."

"Two," I replied.

"Two?" he said, leveling his gun at me, but I could tell he was not ready to use it yet. My eyesight had returned to normal. "Well, two out of six ain't so bad."

Six? I thought to myself. This was new news. He looked over at the desk. "I know you are back there, whoever you are, I can smell you too. Stand up."

Juan stood up slowly and moved from behind the desk so he had a clear path to the man.

"Well, Reverend Billy John will want to talk to you both. Come on over here." He motioned to Juan with his gun. Juan had barely begun to comply when I felt the night watchman's aura change.

Danger Close!

The night watchman had suddenly realized Juan had moved from behind the desk and was now a threat. He had decided to shoot him, I could feel the level of anger change in the man's aura. I had to act now, but I was prepared. I'd known all along it was going to come to this. Right now, I had to protect Juan's life, and I knew it had to be immediately.

I took the single necessary step to close the distance and "snap kicked" him in in the elbow of the arm holding the gun, knocking it up where it no longer pointed at Juan. He began to bring the gun down and turned toward me. I used a "snap punch" with the heel of my hand into the base of his nose. This disconnects the nasal cartilage from the skull and drives it up into the frontal lobe of the brain and kills your opponent instantly if properly executed.

My snap punch was properly executed. He was dead before his body hit the ground.

Juan looked at me and shrugged. "It had to be done, Mary Ellyn. I felt the changes too."

We wrestled the man's body through the window. "What now?" I asked as I noticed the little red light was off and removed the Memory Stick.

"Well," Juan replied, "Let's get the glass back in and then take his body back into the woods somewhere. The spring turkey season is over. No one will be around to find the body until the fall deer season."

"And anyway, there's no way to trace it back to us if he is found," I pointed out. "Can you carry him?"

After replacing the glass, he threw the night watchman's dead body over his shoulder without a lot of effort. "Yes," he said with a thin supportive smile. I understood. I had just killed the man. The range of emotions that sets off in you is never pleasant. I knew. So did Juan.

He carried the body back through the forest to the logging road. "Let's move it back in a ways," he suggested, "on the other side." We took the body back into the forest on the opposite side of the road another hundred yards or so. Juan dropped it to the ground. It fell with an unceremonious thud.

We had no shovel, and no real desire to bury the body anyway. "Let's burn his clothing and scatter the ashes. Leave the body for the bears, and the razorbacks," I suggested. "It may never get discovered at all."

"Fitting," Juan agreed. "One of us should drive his car and leave it in a strip club's parking lot. That will raise a lot of questions." We made our way back to our car, I drove it, and Juan drove the night watchman's back to town. We left it in the parking lot of a well-attended strip club.

As we started back to our hotel, Juan immediately called Helena and Charley. They had to know about the other four attackers, and what we'd done with the night watchman.

"We had four more attacks, guys," Helena reported rather somberly before Juan could even tell them what had happened or what we had learned. "Two here and two at our Portillo, Chile resort."

"Did they get any of us?" I asked immediately.

"Two," Helena answered soberly. "One here, and one in Chile. The one here was a guest." We had not completed the security system changeover. "Will paralyzed the guest's attacker, and the guest is in surgery right now, but those are the only details I have at the moment. I don't know the guest's condition yet. How are you, guys, are you OK?"

"Yes," Juan answered and explained what we'd learned, and ended with had been done with their night watchman. As we were still on the phone with Helena, Charley informed us that the virus was active, and they were copying the hard drive. He also told Helena he was looking into something alarming but didn't have enough info yet. That resonated with my Aphrodite Intuition. I knew this was not going to be the end of all of this, just the beginning, and more bad news was coming. I explained what my intuition was telling me to Juan as we were driving back to the hotel.

"You know," he said thoughtfully, "None of our priestesses have ever had to use your Aphrodite Intuition in a situation of real danger like this before. It's a real advantage."

About an hour later, we got to our room, and I looked at my watch. It was not even ten o'clock. I had barely sat down on the recliner when we heard my cell phone ring. It was a group video call with both Helena and Charley.

"Three things," Charley began with a grave tone to his voice. "First, they have kidnapped five girls from Arkansas State College."

"What?" came exploding out of my mouth unbidden, and a look of concern spread across Juan's face.

"Yeah," Charley confirmed. "They took them last night. The girls they targeted were wearing "especially suggestive clothing in singles bars' to quote them." He paused, then continued, "As bad as this is, the second thing is just as bad." He exhaled a heavy sigh.

"Next Friday," Charlie continued, "they have targeted five singles bars in the Hot Springs area. They are going to send two members into each bar, one for security, and the other to 'pick up the most suggestively dressed girl in there,' to quote their plan outline, and kidnap her too."

"That's ten girls in total." I gasped. "What are they going to do with them?"

"That's the third thing. It's the worst part. They are going to live stream their rapes and executions," Helena spat out. "On the dark web. They're using it as a fund raiser. Their goal is to raise ten million dollars."

Juan and I looked at each other. We were stunned.

"Somewhere along the way they seem to have come to understand that harassing us is not going to have the impact they want," Helena continued. "They intend to up their game."

"They think they can sell at least a hundred thousand tickets," Charley said with obvious bitterness in his voice, "at one hundred dollars each."

"People would pay to see something like that?" I blurted out.

"Every pervert on the planet is on the dark web," Charley explained, the combination of disgust and sadness clear in his voice. "They will sell more tickets than that."

"Their website says they've already sold over twenty thousand," Helena said sadly, "and that is not the last thing."

"There's something else?" Juan asked the anger evident in the tone of his voice.

"Yes," Charley answered. "There are going to use the money to essentially disperse and disappear into four man cells around the country. Then they are going to buy a lot of advertising announcing that these first ten killings are just the beginning. Any woman who does not dress modestly and acknowledge the authority of her husband over her or, if she's unmarried, her father, may expect to be attacked."

Neither Juan nor I knew what to say. My Aphrodite Intuition had alerted me to the idea this was going to get worse, but I didn't realize it would be this bad.

"Sort of like Brian said," Juan noted, then paused and parsed his lips. "This is terrorism."

"Yes," Helena agreed, "but terror is how a lot of people believe they can draw attention to something no one would consider otherwise. People only resort to terror when they know they can't win any other way."

More silence.

"We can't allow this," I finally blurted out. "But the way we got our info means we can't share this with the FBI."

"Of course not, Mary Ellyn," Helena agreed. "The first thing is to release the girls they have, and prevent more from being taken, or the other way around maybe. Once we do free both groups, we can disappear, and those girls can go to the FBI."

"We are sending four more MA instructors," Charley interjected, "along with four more Sam Dan level priestesses up to you. You five priestesses will be the bait. You'll be the most suggestively dressed girls in the bar."

"Five pairs along with you, guys," Helena interjected, "assuming that you're willing."

"Can you imagine us not being?" I asked bitterly.

"No," Helena agreed with a thin serious smile, "but you know I had to ask."

"We are going to break this up," Charley continued. "We are developing a plan and will text you the addresses of these bars. We want you two to spend an evening in each and case them out. Be friendly, take some pictures, play the out of town tourists. Get us the layouts of those bars. We will also get you the address of the location of the five girls. We need you to scout that area too."

"Other than that, guys," Helena cautioned, "just wait. Help is on the way."

Chapter Thirteen

Juan and I just looked at each other, and I knew we were both thinking the same thing. "Mon Cheri Amour," I began, "It is going to be really hard for me to just sit here and wait. I know scouting all of this out is important, but doing nothing else is going to be hard."

Juan nodded pensively. One of the things I loved about him was he was not a sidelines kind of man. He was a do something kind of man, just like I was a do something kind of woman.

"I know," he nodded. "And we might find something else we can do. If a good opportunity presents itself, we should take it, but the key has to be making sure we don't get discovered and blow this. Ten people's lives are at risk."

It was my turn to nod pensively. "OK, I know you're right. So, as hard as it may be, the first thing is not to do something stupid, just so we have something to do."

"Right. Our first rule has to be to do no harm. Do you feel like starting on these bars tonight?" Juan asked. "Because the energy I have left; I would like to give to you." He walked over to me, put his hands on my waist and gently kissed me, almost like before. Just as gentle, but this time I knew he was kissing the girl he loved with his whole heart.

This was *Eros* + *Agape* love. We both knew it and we both knew our partner knew it too.

"No," I answered, "I don't want to start tonight." I kissed back the man I loved with my whole heart.

He nodded and smiled another thin smile, but there was something else we had to do before we got to that. Killing someone is never a victory. It may be the best possible outcome under the circumstances, but not a victory, a significant piece of your soul is damaged and if not healed, in time it will atrophy. That's the thing about violence of any kind, physical, verbal, economic, whatever. It makes no difference what motivated the violence, it poisons your soul a little, and if you don't get the poison out, before long violence will take you over. It may be that what started out as 'justice' or 'good' or 'they had it coming' may well have been true, but when it takes you over it does not stay good. It morphs into a quest for power which will eventually make you evil and if you don't pursue power, it sinks you into the blackness of depression.

I had killed a man today.

The Zen process for healing your soul was what I had needed before, and Juan helped me. It was what I needed now. I had killed a man with one punch. It makes no difference how 'just' my motive was. The night watchman worked for a group willing to promote their view of righteousness, by doing wickedness, and he intended to kill Juan. Preventing that was certainly 'just,' but still, a man was dead by my hand.

This time I did not need Juan to encourage me to let it all out. I opened up to my wonderful lover easily and we talked it all through, until I had said everything I needed to say.

The poison was out. Now what I needed to finish healing was the soothing part. This became Juan's show and we both knew this too.

He caressed my cheek with the back of his hand. We moved from the couch to the bed. He lay me down and began to kiss me and stroke my face and neck. That was all, for a long time. Just gentle soft kisses and sensuous caresses.

After about an hour, I got up, kissed him softly, and began a slow strip tease. We were still in the black outfits we'd worn. I crossed my arms and pulled my top up over my head, shook out my hair and, while doing a slow girl shimmy, slid my jeans down off of my hips and slowly down to my ankles. I stepped out of them, unfastened and removed my bra, then slid my panties down into a pile near my jeans.

I lay back down on the bed, his naked girl in all her glory.

Juan rose and stripped for me. I watched his pecks, his shoulders, arms, and six pack flex as he eased out of his shirt. Then I enjoyed the luscious treat of admiring the firmness of his ass and legs as he slipped out of his jeans. I got a nice look at his package still wrapped in his jockey shorts as he stepped out of the jeans, and then his majestic stiff Cock as he took off the shorts.

He lay down next to me, my naked guy in all his glory.

He took one of my breasts into his mouth, and the other with his hand and began to massage them. After a bit, his hand drifted down to my Venus Mons, and he did a Venus Massage there for a nice long time.

This time, as we savored each other, I noticed the flavor was different, better. I wondered why for a moment and then realized... this was *Eros + Agape,* no wonder it was better. The flavor of savoring *Eros* was magnificent of itself, but when *Eros + Agape* were interwoven, savoring the combination was stratospheric.

Then he ran his finger down my Labia to my Intro, brought nectar up to my Hot Spot and very lightly, massaged me there too. The point was to be soothing, not exciting, and Juan was exceptionally good at it all.

After a while, he found his way between my legs and entered me. We did Full Sensation Thrusts for another hour or so, shared our orgasms and he kept the Afterglow Orgasm going until we were spent.

As we lay there, two individual people but one indivisible entity, I knew this was different now. Not that there was anything inferior about what we'd shared before, but something profound had happened between the two of us. A trade had been made. It was not one either one of us had planned, but it happened, nonetheless.

Juan finally rolled over and looked into my eyes, "You know there's no one but you for me now. I love you, only you."

"I know," I replied softly, "I love you too, only you."

My heart had given me to Juan. It had not asked my mind for permission; it had not counted the cost or made any plans; it had just given me away. I was Juan's and there was gladness ringing in my heart. Being with another man was no longer something that I could imagine. One hundred percent of the *Eros + Agape* love I had in me would be focused on this man.

Likewise, Juan's heart had given him to me without consulting his head either. Other women were now out of the question for him too. One hundred percent of his *Eros* + *Agape* love would be focused on me.

His mind was no more involved than mine. Whatever plans were needed, interrupted, or modified were irrelevant. Juan was mine; I was his, and that was that. He wasn't fighting either and was just as glad as me, and the truth was, this made my heart sing.

Whether we were ready or not was no longer relevant. Our love had evolved beyond those sorts of questions. It was still *Eros* love. We would have that forever, but now, *Agape* love had formed firmly around our *Eros* love. What I felt for this wonderful man was the unconditional love on which permanent relationships are founded, and all I wanted now was the single focus on one man that excluded all others. He was clearly in the same place.

Did Aphrodite work her magic on us? Yes, of course she did. This is one of her great lessons. For many people this jump into commitment can be hard. For us it was easy, and the reason is simple enough when you think it through. *Eros* love is an intermediate commitment, but it does involve a commitment.

You are committing to be everything you can be for him; he is committing to be everything he can be for you, one day at a time. This is an intermediate step, one that is easy and fun to take. You get used to keeping your commitment and he reaps the reward, and likewise with him. He keeps his and you reap the reward, and you both learn that real commitments… kept… work out well for both of you.

If you've loved and lost a time or two, it is normal to be afraid. But when you are making *Eros* love with someone, your natural fear is replaced by knowledge. The thing is you both can evaluate how well you and your partner are doing at keeping your commitments, and if you're both doing well, the next step is just a natural evolution, not a giant leap. And you learn what is perhaps Aphrodite's greatest lesson. You learn *Eros* love is the best possible place to start, but then, evolving into an *Eros* + *Agape* relationship is the only way to get the best from life.

Learning these lessons made it easy for Juan and me. We were filled with the wonder called love, *Eros* + *Agape* love. And the changes coming to our lives did not feel like something lost, rather like a page turned to discover the beginning of a new Chapter where much was to be gained.

We could consider becoming priestess and priest on the couple's side. Or Juan and I could go off and start the bakery that Shannel and I had dreamed of. Or find another path, any other path, that suited us both. There were still many unanswered questions, but the central one for Juan and me was now answered.

Together we would find a way to deal with whatever came. We both knew it, but there was a dangerous evil in this land, and good people needed to take a stand. Light will, in the end, always defeat darkness, provided good people are willing to stand up and hold their torches high. Juan and I would do our part, and if the Heavens were with us, come out the other side.

The End of the Beginning.

Afterward

May your life be seasoned with the delicious presence of Aphrodite, the Divine Feminine by whatever name you choose. May the Heavens bless you richly above all you can ask or think and may every dream of *Eros* + *Agape* love you ever dreamed, come true. Amen!

I would like to make it clear that I am not promoting any particular religious group. I am a Christian, an Anglican. (Episcopalian in North America) This is where I get the meat and potatoes for my relationship with God. I season this with the Divine Feminine. I believe you should do whatever feeds your soul.

All of the techniques for making *Eros* love described here are real. If you have tried them as you read this book, you already know. If not, I wonder why. Try them for yourself, you'll see. Some take a bit more "practice" than others, so keep at it. Once you're there, share them shamelessly with your friends. The joys of the fruit offered by Aphrodite are for everyone.

As neat as the idea of the Diving Bell is, and it certainly can be done with currently available technology, do not try and build one without the help of a Mechanical Engineer experienced with diving equipment. You can kill yourself this way, so if you want one, work with a professional.

As enticing as a threesome with a forest is, until you and your lover are adept at *Eros* love, can merge your auras into a Love Bubble, and find the Doorstep to Heaven, you should concentrate on mastering this first. All it takes is a lot of the most wonderful "practice" on earth. After you find your way to the Doorstep a few times, have a great time in the forest.

Aphrodite Intuition is real. The way a woman develops hers is exactly as presented here. Just so you know, a woman in the work place, adept at Aphrodite Intuition, will know where her boss is going sometimes before she or he does, always before her co-workers do, additionally she will have a far easier time solving difficult problems quickly. If developed, Aphrodite Intuition is an incredible advantage for a woman. Did you honestly believe the Goddess would have allowed men to be given men the advantages they receive from testosterone, without giving women similar advantages?

The 'Foundation for Righteousness is not based on any specific group. The use of a group like the "Foundation for Righteousness" is not a religious statement, or an indictment of anyone's religious beliefs. It is a metaphor for every group or individual that believes a good end can be achieved through deeds that harm others. It can't! To those of you involved with the Cancel Culture, Environmental Activism or any political movements, I am specifically speaking to you. Your goals may well be noble, but whenever you hurt someone else, you damage a piece of your soul. Noble goal or not is irrelevant. Self-congratulation or the admiration of those who agree with you will not heal it. This damage will warp your judgement and eventually ruin your life. Lofty goals cannot be achieved by taking the low road. It does not lead where lofty goals live. High goals are achieved by a long trudge up the high road. It is hard, but all lofty goals live in high places, and the high road of undebatably sound logic and non-violence is the only way to get there. Whatever your goals are, I suggest you take that road.

Stay tuned... there is much more to say about Aphrodite, her lessons and Fantasy Bay.